"Hello, my name is Cici. I'm happy you came to our service today."

Jimmy stared into her eyes as he held the soft, gloved hand in his. He hadn't been dreaming. She really was the most beautiful woman he'd ever seen.

"Not as happy as I am." Hardly knowing what he was doing, he lifted her hand and placed a soft kiss on the gloved fingers, then lifted his eyes and looked into hers.

A blush colored her cheeks and her lips turned up in a slightly shocked smile. "A chivalrous deed," she said. "A trifle bold, perhaps, but I think I liked it."

"Forgive me. I couldn't restrain myself."

"Well, we'd better go. Good-bye, Cici." Eddy grabbed Jimmy's arm and practically dragged him away.

Jimmy followed as though in a daze. Had he actually kissed her hand? "Why did we have to leave so fast?" he objected as they walked down the street.

"For your own protection."

"What?"

"If I'd known she was going to have that effect on you, I'd never have introduced you." He gave Jimmy a pitying look.

"What are you talking about, you idiot?"

"Cici is Rev. Willow's daughter, and she devours love-smitten fellows like you. One minute she's all sweet and girly; then the next she's giving a fellow a tongue-lashing. Sort of like sugar and spice, you know?"

FRANCES DEVINE spent most of her childhood, teen, and young adult years in Dallas, Texas, but lived for five years in a little country community called Brushy Creek among the beautiful pine woods of East Texas. There, she wrote her first story at the age of nine. She moved to Southwest Missouri more than twenty years ago and fell in love with the hills, the fall colors, and Silver Dollar City. Frances considers herself blessed to have the opportunity to write for Barbour Publishing. She is the mother of seven adult children and has fourteen wonderful grandchildren. Frances is happy to hear from her fans. E-mail her at fd1440writes@aol.com.

Books by Frances Devine

HEARTSONG PRESENTS
HP847—A Girl Like That
HP871—Once a Thief

Sugar
and Spice

Frances Devine

Heartsong Presents

With love, to my children and grandchildren. And to my precious
great-grands, Lauryn, Braylon, and Christopher. Special thanks
to JoAnne Simmons, my editor at Heartsong, who gave me the
opportunity to honor the victims of the Eastland disaster while
writing a story of love and family. And my heartfelt gratitude to
Aaron McCarver who helps me to make my books so much better.
To the city of Chicago itself for its history and its people. To my
faithful friends who encourage me and pray for me. To my readers
who make this possible. Most of all, to my Lord, Jesus Christ, who
loves unconditionally and forgives freely.

A note from the Author:
*I love to hear from my readers! You may correspond with
me by writing:*

> **Frances Devine**
> **Author Relations**
> **PO Box 721**
> **Uhrichsville, OH 44683**

ISBN 978-1-60260-706-4

SUGAR AND SPICE

All scripture quotations are taken from the King James Version of the
Bible.

All of the characters and events in this book are fictitious. Any resem-
blance to actual persons, living or dead, or to actual events is purely
coincidental.

*Our mission is to publish and distribute inspirational products offering
exceptional value and biblical encouragement to the masses.*

PRINTED IN THE U.S.A.

one

Chicago, January 1915

Snow crunched under Jimmy's feet as he crossed the street to Nelsons' Law Firm. The cold late February wind whipped around his neck. Jimmy raised his collar against it and hoped Blake's response to his announcement wouldn't be as chilly.

Miss Howard, the firm's secretary, smiled sweetly. "Good morning, Mr. Grayson. Nasty weather, isn't it?"

"I'm ready for spring." Jimmy unbuttoned his coat. "Can I go on back?"

"Yes, he's expecting you."

Jimmy went through the swinging gate and headed down the hall to his brother-in-law's office, repeating in his head the words he'd practiced. He took a deep breath. Blake had always been kind to him, and he had no reason to think this time would be different. Except that Danni wasn't going to like the news, and Blake didn't like it when his wife was upset.

He tapped on the door and entered Blake's neat office. The smell of leather and Murphy's oil greeted his nostrils as he closed the door and stepped up to Blake's desk.

"Hi, Jimmy." Blake looked up and lifted his eyebrows. "What's so important it couldn't wait until after work?"

"I need to talk to you first, without Danni."

An amused smile crinkled Blake's face. "Uh-oh, it must be bad if you don't want your sister to know about it."

Jimmy swallowed hard. This wasn't going to be easy. "I want you to know. . ." He cleared his throat and started again. "Blake, you know how much I appreciate everything you've done for me. And I know Danni has her heart set on my

5

continuing in your footsteps." He paused.

A cautious look crossed Blake's face, but he remained silent.

"I've enjoyed my year and a half at law school, but."

Blake stood up behind his desk. "Are you saying you don't want to be an attorney?"

Jimmy licked his lips and searched Blake's eyes. No condemnation. At least, not yet. Jimmy's shoulders relaxed. "I'm just not sure." Jimmy dropped into the chair in front of the desk, and Blake returned to his.

"I see."

"I like law. And I want to help people. I also know how much you've spent on my education this far."

Blake waved the comment away.

"Lately, I've felt there's something missing. Something I can't put my finger on."

"What is it, exactly, you want to do?"

"I'm not sure. Maybe I'll end up getting my law degree. But I need to know for certain." Jimmy hesitated. "I'd like to take a semester off." He leaned forward, awaiting his brother-in-law's reaction.

"And you think you'll find your answers in a semester?"

"I don't know, but I have to try." Jimmy gave Blake a steady look. "If I don't return to law school, I promise I'll pay back every cent you've spent. And don't think I'm going to live off you and Danni while I'm searching. I'll get a job to pay my own way."

"Money isn't what's important here, Jimmy."

"I know. But I'll feel better."

Blake inhaled deeply and tapped a pencil on his desk. "I wish you'd think about it a little bit longer. Maybe talk to your instructors at school, or even Rev. Martin."

Jimmy bit his lip. Why had everything seemed so reasonable a few minutes ago but now, under Blake's scrutiny, didn't?

"I have spoken to two of my professors about my doubts."

"And?"

Jimmy sighed. "They tried to talk me out of it. But Blake, this isn't just a whim. It's something I feel I must do. As much as I enjoy law, my heart isn't in it."

Blake sat back in his chair and once more tapped the pencil against his desk. Suddenly he sat up and grinned at Jimmy. "Did you know I once left the firm to write musical comedy?"

"Sure. The one Danni was in."

"That's right. My father was furious for a while. So who am I to stop another man from searching his heart? Don't worry about Danielle. I'll talk to her." Blake stood and held out his hand. "After all, you're twenty years old. It's time she realized that."

"Thanks, Blake. I hope she won't be too upset." Jimmy rose and took Blake's hand.

As he left the building, relief washed over him and he felt free for the first time in months. A light snow had begun to fall again. Jimmy stood for a moment, wondering what his next move should be. The warehouses near Clark Street, over by the docks, were always hiring. He started down the street toward the livery where he'd left his horse and buggy.

Ahead, two young women stepped out of a department store, arms full of packages. But Jimmy's attention fell upon only one. Golden blond hair, topped with a tiny blue-feathered hat, fanned out across the collar of her blue wool coat. As she reached him, a parcel fell from her arms.

Jimmy picked it up and held it out to her as though presenting a gift to a queen.

Lovely blue eyes sparkled at him as her lips curved into a pouty smile. "Thank you, sir." Her musical words rippled through him and he caught his breath. She passed by, before he could think of a word to say, and continued down the sidewalk.

Jimmy turned and stared after the vision, hardly aware of her companion. He'd never seen such a beautiful girl.

The angry voice of a man shoving by him jerked Jimmy back to attention. Shaking himself, he laughed and continued down the street to the livery.

Jimmy, you idiot. She's just a girl.

Turning the corner, he stopped at the stable and got his horse and buggy, then crossed the bridge and left them at a nearby livery. If he got a job in the area, he'd ride the streetcar to work. It was time he got around like the rest of the working class. He headed down the dirt street beside the Chicago River. Clumps of floating ice didn't stop the barges lined up at the dock, loading and unloading their goods.

Jimmy looked around, and a wave of nausea hit him as memories of his childhood came flooding back. He could easily find his way to the house where he'd first met Sutton, the man who'd held him and his sister captive for eight years, convincing them he was looking out for them.

Resisting a sudden urge to run, Jimmy forced himself to continue down the street to the warehouses. A little girl in a threadbare coat ran by, laughing. Her mane of blond curls caused him to think of the beauty he'd helped earlier that day. He wondered if he'd ever see her again. Probably not. There were a lot of people in Chicago. So how could he expect to see those gorgeous eyes and tantalizing lips again? He grinned and headed toward the nearest warehouse.

☙

Cici sat beside Helen on the slatted seat of the streetcar and cast a sideways glance at her friend, who shook her head and grinned.

"What?" Cici looked at her with wide-eyed innocence.

"What indeed." Helen shook her head again. "That was bold, my friend."

Cici laughed. "Okay. I dropped it on purpose. But how else was I to get his attention?"

"How?" Helen hooted with laughter. "Since when have you needed to try to get a man's attention? You already have all the young men of our acquaintance smitten. Leave a few for the rest of us, dear."

"Oh, don't be modest. Eddy Wright doesn't know I'm around when you're in the room."

"Okay, so one young man is impervious to your charm." Helen blushed. "Eddy is rather special. I'm glad he notices me."

Cici sighed. "I wonder if I'll ever see him again."

"Who? Eddy?" Helen looked at her in surprise. "You see him every Sunday at church."

"No, silly. I mean *him*. The man who picked up my package."

"Hmm. It looks like the tables were turned this time. So he got your attention, too." Helen nodded. "Serves you right."

Cici giggled softly. "He *was* handsome though. Did you notice those dark brown eyes?"

The girls chattered until they reached Cici's stop then said good-bye.

Cici walked the half block to the parsonage, struggling to hang on to her packages. Why in the world hadn't she taken a cab? She wrestled the packages through the front door, letting the screen door slam behind her.

"Is that you, Cici, dear?" Her mother's voice seemed to sing the words.

"Yes, Mama." Cici dropped the packages on the rug in the parlor and flopped down on the sofa, breathing hard.

"Goodness, you had your arms full." Caroline Willow came through the door from the kitchen, drying her hands on a dishcloth. "You didn't take the streetcar, did you?"

"Yes, I don't know what I was thinking."

"Well, get out of your coat and go change clothes. I'll make you a hot cup of tea. We have to bake for the Community Bazaar."

"All right. Just let me get my breath a minute."

"I don't know how you stand to ride those noisy streetcars. The one time I tried it, I felt absolutely nauseous."

After she'd changed and returned to the kitchen, Cici stood for a moment and watched her mother cutting sugar cookies. "Mama, don't you ever wish your life was more exciting?"

Mama chuckled. "I think it's exciting enough. We have to bake a dozen pies and six dozen cookies." She opened the oven door and put the pan of cookies inside.

"But that's not what I mean, Mama." Cici realized her voice had taken on a hint of exasperation, and she softened her tone. "Baking and cleaning and ironing. Don't you get sick of it sometimes?"

Her mother turned and gave her a puzzled look. "No, dear. I never get sick of it. Tired, sometimes, but I wouldn't trade my life for anything."

"Well, I want more out of *my* life." Cici gave a small stamp of her foot on the floor. Then realizing what she'd done, she reached over and put her arm around her mother's shoulders. "I'm sorry, Mama."

Mama smoothed Cici's hair back off her forehead. A small frown appeared on the older woman's face. "Cecilia," she said softly, "I don't know why God gave you such an adventurous spirit, but you can be sure He wants to use it for His glory. Wait on Him. Don't do anything rash. You aren't a little child anymore. You're a young lady of eighteen."

Cici leaned into her mother's hand and smiled. "My escapades gave you a lot of grief, didn't they, Mama?"

"You've never given me grief." Her mother spoke tenderly. "Worry maybe, but not grief."

Cici giggled. "Remember the time I turned Mrs. Gardner's chickens loose?"

"I think that's best forgotten, my dear, as well as the time you decided to whitewash Mr. Taylor's milk cow."

"He was so angry. But not nearly as angry as Mrs. Potts was when I put the garter snake in her desk drawer."

"That was very naughty, and the school almost lost a teacher over it. Which is what I meant when I said you should wait on Him. He can fulfill your need for adventure without your bringing grief to others."

"I thought you said I've never brought you grief." Cici's eyes danced.

"Well, you haven't. But you certainly brought grief to a lot of others."

"Papa might say I bring him grief."

"Grief? What have you been up to now, Cecilia?"

Cici glanced up as her father walked into the kitchen. "Not a thing, Papa." Cici stood on tiptoe and gave her father a kiss on the cheek.

"How is Mrs. Appleby, George?" Mama took Papa's coat and laid it on a kitchen chair.

"Not too well, I'm afraid." Rev. Willow kissed his wife on the forehead. "The doctor isn't sure she'll make it through the night."

"I'm so sorry, dear." She patted her husband on the cheek. "But at least we know where she's going. She's served the Lord faithfully for many years. I think she wants to go on to a better life."

Grabbing the last of the batch of dough, Cici rolled out a pie shell and placed it into a pan. As she mixed dough for another batch, she tuned her parents out and let her mind wander back to her morning. She smiled as she thought of the young man on the sidewalk. A lock of dark brown hair had fallen across his forehead as he bent to retrieve her package. But it was the look in his dark eyes that had piqued her curiosity. Excitement. Or perhaps anticipation of something about to happen. She wondered if she'd ever see him again.

two

Jimmy grunted as he lifted his end of a gigantic crate and swung it over to rest on top of another.

"Whew." Eddy Wright wiped his forehead with a sleeve and grinned at Jimmy. "You're getting broken in the hard way today."

Bending over and resting his hands on his knees, Jimmy took a deep breath. "What's in these crates anyway?"

"I've no idea. Our job is to move them, not to look inside." Eddy moved to the next crate, motioning for Jimmy to pick up the other end.

The first few days on the job had been fairly easy, but the night before, this new shipment had come in. Jimmy had a new respect for the men who worked here day and night, practically all their lives.

After they had deposited the crate in its new location, they headed for their lunch break.

"Come on. Let's go watch the boats unload while we eat." Eddy grabbed his lunch bucket and Jimmy followed suit. His new friend, whose cheerful conversation had made the morning easier to handle, had stirred Jimmy's curiosity. Obviously no stranger to this sort of work, or to the neighborhood, he spoke in a way that proved him to be educated and well mannered.

A twinge of sadness hit Jimmy as he sat on an upended barrel and ate his lunch. The docks brought bad memories from his childhood, but he had earlier memories from before his mother died. Good memories of walks by the river and a soft hand holding on to his. Or were they really memories?

Perhaps they were merely desires buried deep in his heart. He'd been so young. He should probably ask Danni. But he'd rather hang on to the memories, real or not.

A group of children ran up to Eddy, chattering and laughing. He laid his sandwich aside and gave all his attention to them. At one boy's joke, he threw back his head and roared with laughter. He opened his lunch bucket and looked inside. "Hmm, what's this in my lunch pail, I wonder." Reaching inside, he pulled out a paper parcel, which proved to contain cheese and sausages. He passed them out to the children, who bowed their heads and waited until Eddy had said grace.

Jimmy watched the children as they ate, thanked Eddy, and then ran off to play. "Do you do this often?" he asked.

"I try to at least twice a week. They're hungry, you know."

"Yes. . ." Jimmy felt his voice break. "I do know."

Eddy looked at him, curiosity on his face.

"My sister and I were orphaned when we were very young. I remember the pangs of hunger quite well."

"I'm sorry to hear that."

The old wounds had healed long ago, but the sincerity in Eddy's voice was like ointment flowing over the scar tissue that still ached at times. "Thank you. It was long ago, and we're fine now. We were luckier than most." With a rueful shake of his head, he added, "No one ever gave us lunch though. Not willingly, at least. Why do you do this?"

Eddy smiled. "God told me to."

"Oh." He gave a little laugh. "Now you sound like my sister, Danni. She says God talks to her, too."

"Do you attend church?"

"Yes, I go with my sister and her husband. Why?"

"What sort of minister do you have there?"

"Oh, the usual sort, I suppose." Now why would Eddy ask that? "You know, he talks about God, like he should."

Eddy chuckled. "That's good."

"Why do you ask?"

"Oh, I thought you might like to try mine some Sunday. It's a great church and you'd be welcome."

"What's so great about it?" After all, a church was a church.

Eddy smiled. "For one thing, our minister, Rev. Willow, is a godly man who loves to share life-changing sermons. Also," he said with a grin, "a lot of pretty girls attend."

Jimmy nodded solemnly. "Uh-huh. I see. Well, I might just have to try it out. . .for the sermons, of course."

The following Sunday found Jimmy seated next to Eddy in the small stone church. He'd been introduced to the reverend and several others, but so far no girls.

Just as Rev. Willow took the podium, Jimmy heard a scurrying and a young woman hurried down the aisle and sat in the second pew. His stomach lurched at the sight of golden blond curls.

Come on, Jimmy, what are the chances? There are probably hundreds of girls with hair just that shade.

Jimmy tried to focus on the hymn they were singing, and by the time the sermon started, he'd convinced himself the young woman in the second pew couldn't possibly be the girl he had dreamed about for the past week and a half.

Eddy was right about Rev. Willow. Jimmy didn't remember any sermon touching his soul this way before.

After the service, Jimmy glanced at the young woman as she stood and turned. His breath caught in his throat. He reached over and grabbed Eddy's sleeve, tugging frantically.

"What?" Eddy pulled his sleeve out of Jimmy's grasp.

"Do you know that girl?" Jimmy whispered.

Eddy glanced over and grinned. "Sure, I know her. Why?"

"Will you introduce us?"

"I might, for a price." He was enjoying this too much.

"Name it."

"Hey, I was only kidding. Come on."

Eddy led the way through the departing church members to where she stood.

As they approached, she smiled at Eddy. "Hi, Eddy. If you're looking for Helen, she's home with a cold." She glanced briefly in Jimmy's direction then lowered her eyes, her long lashes fluttering against her cheeks.

"I know." He threw a sideways glance at Jimmy. "Actually, I came to say hello to you and to introduce you to my friend, Jimmy Grayson."

She lifted her glance to Jimmy, her lips curving in an adorable little smile, and held out her hand. "Hello, my name is Cici. I'm happy you came to our service today."

Jimmy stared into her eyes as he held the soft, gloved hand in his. He hadn't been dreaming. She really was the most beautiful woman he'd ever seen.

"Not as happy as I am." Hardly knowing what he was doing, he lifted her hand and placed a soft kiss on the gloved fingers, then lifted his eyes and looked into hers.

A blush colored her cheeks and her lips turned up in a slightly shocked smile. "A chivalrous deed," she said. "A trifle bold, perhaps, but I think I liked it."

"Forgive me. I couldn't restrain myself."

"Well, we'd better go. Good-bye, Cici." Eddy grabbed Jimmy's arm and practically dragged him away.

Jimmy followed as though in a daze. Had he actually kissed her hand? "Why did we have to leave so fast?" he objected as they walked down the street.

"For your own protection."

"What?"

"If I'd known she was going to have that effect on you, I'd never have introduced you." He gave Jimmy a pitying look.

"What are you talking about, you idiot?"

"Cici is Rev. Willow's daughter, and she devours love-smitten fellows like you. One minute she's all sweet and girly; then the next she's giving a fellow a tongue-lashing. Sort of like sugar and spice, you know?"

❧

Helen sat straight up on her bed, then moaned and leaned

back onto her pillows. "Are you kidding me?" She coughed. "It was the same man?"

Cici nodded. "The very same."

Helen's eyes widened and she grabbed a hanky from her bedside table and sneezed loudly.

"Goodness, maybe I'd better leave so you can rest."

"No, don't you dare. Tell me everything. Do you mean to say he kissed your hand, right there in church, with everyone looking on?"

"Mm-hmm," Cici said in a dreamy voice. "Well, not everyone. Nearly everyone had left, but I think Papa may have seen."

"Oh no. Did he say anything?" Helen's red-rimmed eyes rounded with excitement.

"Not yet." A niggling of worry bit at Cici's mind, but she pushed it away. "Anyway, what could he say? It wasn't my fault Jimmy kissed me."

"Kissed your hand," Helen corrected.

"But it seemed like more." Cici closed her eyes and could almost feel the touch of Jimmy's lips on her hand. She shivered.

"Watch out, Cici." Helen's lips tilted. "I think you've finally fallen for someone."

Cici opened her eyes and sat up. "Oh, it was just the novelty of it all. It was rather romantic though. I wonder if he'll be back."

"I'm going to ask Eddy about him." Helen gave a short but emphatic nod then grabbed another handkerchief and dabbed at her nose. "After all, you don't know the man at all."

"I know. But I don't think Eddy would be friends with someone who wasn't all right. Do you?"

"Well, no, but. . ."

Cici rose and bent to kiss her friend on the forehead. "You take care of that cold. I have to go now. I'm almost late for my appointment at Milady's Coiffure."

Helen sighed, a dreamy look on her face. "You're so lucky. I'd die to have my hair done there."

"Well, perhaps when you turn eighteen next month, your parents will allow it. Like mine did." She grinned. "I think it's their way of turning me from a tomboy to a lady. But I really, really must go. I'll drop by again tomorrow."

"Promise?"

"Promise." Cici gave a little wave and left.

Twenty minutes later, she sat in the chair at Milady's, her hair in tangled knots.

"The things we go through to be beautiful."

Cici turned, curious to see who'd spoken the laughing words. The girl in the next chair appeared to be a little older than Cici. Short brown hair framed a heart-shaped face. Lips pursed in a pretty pout were a little too pink to be natural. Not wishing to appear rude, Cici forced her glance away from the lips and met a pair of gold-flecked green eyes filled with amusement.

"Are you shocked because my lips are painted?"

Cici felt her face grow warm. "I really hadn't noticed," she lied.

The girl chuckled. "All righty, then." She leaned over and held out her hand. "My name is Gail. And you are?"

Cici took the girl's hand. "Cici."

"Well, Cici, lipstick is growing quite popular. Almost everyone uses it now. You should try it."

A little bolt of excitement ran through Cici. To be honest, she'd wanted to try painting her face to see how she would look. "I wouldn't dare," she whispered.

"Why not?" Gail gave her the once-over. "You're quite attractive, but makeup would make you look even better."

"Do you think so?" Cici asked.

"Absolutely. You're very pretty, but with a little lipstick and mascara, you could look like a movie star."

"Oh, I would never use mascara." The very thought seemed

daring yet exciting.

"Well, here, then. Let's try a little color on your lips." Gail slipped off her chair and produced a small cylinder. "Here, pucker your lips like you are about to be kissed."

Unable to resist, Cici closed her eyes and did as directed. Something smooth and moist glided across her lips.

"Now press them together to even it out and see what you think."

Her heart in her throat, Cici opened her eyes and looked in the mirror. Her eyes widened. Gail was right. The lipstick did make her look prettier.

"Well, what do you think? Shall we take it off?" Gail held up tissue.

Cici bit her lip, indecision battling inside her. She couldn't really wear it in public. Could she? "No." Cici held up her hand. "Don't remove it. Thank you very much."

"My pleasure." The girl grinned and sat back on her chair.

Cici took a closer look at her new acquaintance. Actually, Gail seemed quite nice, in spite of her painted face.

Gail chatted endlessly for the next hour and a half while the girls had their hair dressed and nails done. Gail was finished first but continued to chatter to Cici until she, too, was ready to go. By the time they left the salon together, Cici was totally enthralled with her new friend. They agreed to meet somewhere for lunch sometime soon.

"Here." Gail quickly scribbled on a piece of paper and handed it to Cici. "This is my landlady's phone number. I live upstairs. Just ask for me."

Excitement bubbled in Cici as she rode home. She'd never met anyone as intriguing as Gail. A twinge of guilt pinched at her as she thought of Helen, who Cici was sure wouldn't approve of Gail. But she didn't have to know. Cici ignored the second twinge.

As she neared her stop, she grabbed a handkerchief from her pocket and scrubbed, then reached into her handbag and removed a small mirror. Good, there was no sign of the lipstick, but her mouth was red from the scrubbing. She replaced the mirror and stuffed the hankie deep into her handbag, then pulled the bell cord.

She walked the half block home, and as she slipped through the door, her lips curved. What would that daring Jimmy Grayson think of painted lips?

three

Jimmy lifted a heavy crate and stacked it with others intended for the same warehouse. He was glad he'd hired on to work on the docks until noon today. He loved it out here in the open, even with a cold March breeze from the river whipping around his collar. Maybe he should try to find permanent employment here instead of at the warehouse. A steam whistle blew and another boat pulled up.

What was it about this place that kept drawing him back? Children dodged and chased each other as they played on the crowded street. Every now and then, one would get too near the dock and a worker would run him or her off.

Jimmy was getting ready to leave when he saw a small boy being chased off by a stocky laborer who yelled at him to stay away. Something clicked in Jimmy's mind, and he took a closer look at the man. His stomach knotted as though someone had punched him. It was Cobb. The one who'd led Jimmy and Danni to Sutton that cold day so many years ago. Cobb had been a mere boy himself at the time, maybe twelve. By the time Jimmy and his sister were rescued, he must have been twenty or so. He had always been friendly to them, but still, Jimmy felt his heart chill. He turned to leave.

"Hey! Jimbo! Is that you?"

Jimmy groaned and turned to face the man who was sprinting toward him.

Cobb didn't look much different than he did when he was hauled off by the police eight years ago. Cobb grabbed him in a bear hug. "It is you. I can't believe it." He smacked Jimmy on the arm and laughed. "How've you been, kid? How's Danni?"

Jimmy swallowed and attempted a friendly smile. "I'm fine, and Danni's doing well. How about you?"

"Great, just great. I keep busy." He shook his head, grinning widely.

"So how long have you been working here?"

"A couple of years, I guess. Mostly I work in the galley on the *Eastland*. When we're docked, I work here to keep busy."

"They actually pay you to cook?" Jimmy laughed. He could still remember some of Cobb's concoctions; they were pretty bad.

"Yeah, I finally learned you don't add salt to corned beef and you don't put molasses in mashed potatoes." He guffawed.

Jimmy couldn't help grinning back at the friendly face. Why had he even tried to avoid Cobb? After all, he'd been as much a victim of Sutton's as Jimmy and Danni had. And he hadn't gotten off the way they had. He'd served time in prison.

Impulsively, he threw his arm around Cobb's shoulder. "Come on, let's go to lunch somewhere."

"Perfect timing. I just finished loading the *Swallow*. Let me get my stuff." Cobb walked away and was back in five minutes.

They headed down Michigan Avenue, with Cobb continuing to pound Jimmy on the back. "I've missed you, Jimbo. Didn't think I'd ever see you again."

"Yeah, I know. Here, how about this place?"

They entered the diner and found it packed, but they managed to get a table toward the back.

After they had ordered, Cobb glanced at Jimmy, curiosity in his eyes. "So how about you, Jimmy? You working by the docks, too?"

"Yeah, I'm at Henderson's Warehouse."

"Yeah? I worked there a couple of times. Not a bad place. A little surprised to see you there, though. You were always daydreaming. Once that lawyer fellow took you in, I figured you'd get educated."

Jimmy hesitated. "Yes, I went to school. Then college. I'm actually taking a semester off from law school."

Cobb stiffened. "So why are you working as a laborer? Seeing how the lower class lives?"

"That's a dumb thing to say, Cobb," Jimmy retorted. "I grew up here, too, you know."

"Okay, okay. Sorry."

"I took time off to do some soul-searching. I'm just not sure I'm supposed to be a lawyer." He stared at the cup as he stirred sugar into his coffee. "I feel like there's something else I'm supposed to be doing."

Cobb looked puzzled. "Guess I just always figured I'm supposed to do what I have to to get by."

Jimmy nodded, not answering.

"Hey, Jimbo, I noticed you weren't limping. What happened?"

Jimmy hardly remembered anymore that he'd once had a lame foot. "I had an operation. The doctor said if I'd waited much longer, he wouldn't have been able to do much." He took a drink of his coffee. "I still favor it a little when I'm overtired."

"That's great. I thought it might get worse as you grew. Sure glad they could fix it."

Jimmy listened with interest as Cobb regaled him with stories of his adventures at sea. He had a feeling his former friend might be stretching the truth part of the time.

The *Eastland* was leaving the next day for a two-week cruise. They agreed to get together when Cobb returned.

Jimmy took the streetcar home to find a frantic Danni, her auburn curls escaping from the pins that held them back.

"You didn't forget we're having the Kramers and the Robertses over to dinner tonight, did you?"

Jimmy had forgotten, and Danni could read him like a book. As he looked at her frowning face, he grinned. "What can I do to help?"

He spent the rest of the afternoon picking up last-minute items for the dinner and helping Danni with cleaning. As he worked, he thought of the afternoon with Cobb. Should he tell Danni about it?

"Jimmy"—Danni touched his arm—"I have something to tell you. I want you to be one of the first to know."

"What is it?" She'd probably bought something new for the house. She knew she could count on him to praise anything she did around the place.

"Brother, you're going to be an uncle."

Jimmy's mouth fell open and he laughed in delight. He knew his sister had longed for a child. He gave her a gentle hug. "Danni, that's wonderful news. When?"

"Around the first of October." She beamed.

Jimmy felt a tug of emotion at the joy on her face. "You'll be the best mother in the world." And he'd definitely not tell her about Cobb.

"Are you going to services with Blake and me tomorrow," she asked, "or to your friend Eddy's church?"

Jimmy hesitated. And suddenly the adorable face flooded his memories. He'd attended a couple of services with Eddy but had only seen Cici from across the sanctuary. Perhaps that was for the best. He'd tried not to think about her. His future was too up in the air right now to get involved anyway. Maybe he should go with Danni and Blake. But he had promised Rev. Willow he'd be there for the monthly church dinner. "Uh. . .no, I. . .sort of committed to go to Eddy's church tomorrow."

❧

"Is he here?" Cici whispered to Helen. She wasn't about to turn and look, but she was dying to know if Jimmy was here. It had been five weeks since his first visit and he'd only been back twice. But her father had invited Jimmy to the church dinner after today's service and he had promised to come.

"He's coming in now, with Eddy," Helen whispered. "Oh.

They sat down two rows behind us."

"Well, turn around. Don't let him see you looking," Cici whispered fiercely. It wouldn't do to let him think she was watching for him.

Helen giggled and Cici swatted her arm. She didn't know why she was so attracted to Jimmy. He wasn't all that special. Well, he did have those gorgeous big brown eyes. But there was something about him that had caught her attention from the beginning.

She forced herself not to turn around but to focus on her father who was taking his place on the platform. Papa looked quite handsome today, she thought. His dark blue suit was perfectly pressed and his mustache waxed to perfection. He was starting to turn gray at the temples, but Cici thought that made him look very distinguished. She felt a little knot of pride for her father as he smiled and opened his Bible.

She tried to focus on the sermon, but she was too aware of Jimmy two rows behind her. Determined not to let her mind dwell on the handsome young man or the tantalizing kiss he had planted on her hand, she steered her thoughts to her new friend, Gail. Cici had called her a few days before and they'd agreed to meet a week from Tuesday for lunch. She wondered if she dared take the tube of lipstick she'd purchased and hidden in a bureau drawer in a pair of rolled-up stockings. She could apply it after she got on the streetcar. She pushed aside the twinge of guilt and forced herself to listen to her father's sermon. But her thoughts wandered again and again until the congregation stood for a final hymn and then her father closed in prayer.

Picking up her Bible, Cici stepped into the aisle. She and Helen headed for the basement to help set the tables and get the food ready to serve. She used to love church dinners, but for the past couple of years she'd found them boring. Today, however, she felt an excitement she hadn't felt about a church event in a long time.

She'd just served Mr. Gladstone a double portion of mashed potatoes, when out of the corner of her eye she observed Jimmy and Eddy walk in. When they came through the line, she found her hands were trembling.

Jimmy stopped in front of her. "Hi, Cici."

"Oh. Hello, Jimmy. It's nice to see you again." She hoped her voice didn't sound as nervous to him as it did to her own ears.

"It's very nice to see you again, too."

Hmm. He sounded nervous, too. And something else. Was it possible he'd lost interest? Or had she only thought he was interested? Perhaps she should be aloof. It wouldn't do for him to think she cared if he didn't.

"Hi, Helen, Cici. Would you girls join us for lunch?" Eddy asked with a grin.

Helen smiled and nodded. "Thank you. That would be lovely. We'll just be a few more minutes."

Jimmy's eyes found Cici's. He smiled but still had that nervous look on his face. "Is that all right with you, Miss Willow?"

"Yes, I suppose so." She and Helen finished serving then filled their own plates and joined Jimmy and Eddy. She was glad to find that after a few moments with Jimmy, her nervousness disappeared. He seemed to relax also.

After a while, Eddy and Helen wandered off. Cici grew suddenly tongue-tied and groped around for something to say. "What do you think of our little church?"

"I like it a lot. I find Rev. Willow's sermons very inspiring." He glanced across the room to where her parents were visiting with some other couples. She noticed respect in his eyes as he looked at her father.

But she certainly didn't intend to spend the afternoon talking about her father's sermons. "Tell me, Jimmy, what sort of work do you do?"

He hesitated and a trapped look crossed his face; then he relaxed. "To be honest, I'm trying my hand at several things. I work at the warehouse with Eddy through the week. Yesterday I worked on the docks."

"Really? How exciting. My parents won't allow me to go near that district."

"That's probably wise of them. It's no place for a young lady to go alone."

"Tell me about it. What goes on down there?"

"It's usually teeming with people. From passengers boarding steamboats to dockworkers." He smiled. "Children everywhere, and of course there are warehouses and other buildings all along the river. You weren't too far from there the first time I saw you."

"I know, but I was only shopping. Please, tell me more."

She listened, uncomfortable, as Jimmy told her about the poverty of the people who lived in the area.

When Helen and Eddy rejoined them, Cici welcomed them eagerly. She didn't want to hear about poor people. She wanted to hear about adventure and excitement.

The afternoon sped by, and before they knew it, the party was breaking up.

Cici had cornered her parents shortly before and received permission to invite Helen and the boys to dinner the following Sunday.

They all accepted and the boys left, while Cici and Helen helped clean up.

When Cici went to her room that night, she felt happy and eager to see Jimmy again. As she got her night things out, she saw the stockings with the lipstick and suddenly she wasn't sure about her new friendship with Gail. Well, she was going to lunch with her soon. She'd see how she felt about it then. And there really wasn't anything wrong with a little lipstick, was there?

But her conscience answered, *What about deceiving your parents and friends?*

four

"'Commit thy works unto the Lord, and thy thoughts shall be established.'"

Jimmy inhaled sharply, the softly spoken words penetrating his mind and heart like a knife. Did Rev. Willow know about the confusion in his head? But how could he? He hadn't spoken of it to anyone but Blake and Cobb.

"How many times have we skimmed over these words, scarcely noticing them? Do we remember this scripture when we make decisions in our daily lives? Do we even know what the words mean?"

Jimmy leaned forward, eagerness tightening his chest and throat.

"It is really quite simple." Rev. Willow cleared his throat. "It means exactly what it says. Is there an important decision you have to make? Whom to marry. Which house to buy. A career choice."

Yes, yes. But how did he know?

"In these decisions, we must get down on our knees. Discuss the situation with our heavenly Father. Give it to Him. Ask Him what His plan is in the situation. According to God's Word, if we do this, our thoughts shall be established. We will know what to do."

Jimmy frowned and crossed his arms. Was it really that simple? Danni prayed a lot. And Blake always said a blessing over meals. But Jimmy had never really given God much thought other than attending church on Sunday mornings. He wasn't sure he knew how to go about discussing things with God. Maybe he'd get a chance to ask the reverend about it after dinner. He was glad he and Eddy had been invited.

The service over, Jimmy rose. Cici and her friend stood in the aisle by his pew. Startled, he realized he hadn't thought about her during the service even once. Now, as she turned her glance in his direction, he was once more mesmerized by her loveliness.

"Let's go, Jimmy." Eddy shoved him from behind and they moved out into the aisle.

"We may as well walk to the parsonage together, right?" Eddy flashed a grin at the girls.

"Of course." Cici smiled and waited.

"Oh, forgive me." Heat rose in Jimmy's face as he realized the girls were waiting to be escorted. He offered his arm, and Cici slipped her hand inside the crook of his elbow.

The walk to the house next door was much too fast. They stepped inside, and Jimmy felt a twinge of disappointment as Cici removed her hand from his arm.

The girls removed their wraps and went to help Mrs. Willow.

"Come." Rev. Willow motioned toward the chairs by the fireplace. "We might as well visit while we wait."

Supposing this might be the time he could ask the minister about the morning's scripture, Jimmy was a little disappointed when the minister began to regale them with stories from his last hunting trip, then proceeded to tell a joke he'd recently heard. Soon Jimmy found himself roaring with laughter, along with Eddy. Then Cici announced that dinner was served.

They sat down at the food-laden dining table and Rev. Willow stretched his hands out to his wife and daughter, who sat on each side of him. Jimmy, seated next to Cici, took her extended hand as her father blessed the food.

Although he'd expected the dinner conversation to reflect the morning's sermon, the room rang with laughter. Apparently he had a lot to learn about preachers and their families.

After dinner, Rev. Willow invited Eddy and Jimmy to his library. Leather- and cloth-bound volumes lined two walls. Their host walked over to a book-lined shelf.

Jimmy followed. He scanned the titles, but nothing seemed familiar.

"Ah, those are all books on theology." The reverend ran his hand along the spines in an almost caressing manner. He turned and motioned to the book-laden wall across from them. "Those might be more to your liking."

The two younger men followed him across the room.

"*The Three Musketeers.*" Eddy laughed and slipped the book from the shelf. "This was my favorite when I was a lad."

Jimmy found many old friends in the collection, but his eyes kept going back to the shelves on the other wall. He felt drawn to the books and had no idea why. He glanced over and found Rev. Willow studying him with a curious expression on his face.

"Are you interested in theology, Jimmy?" The older man lowered himself into an overstuffed chair and motioned the boys to the sofa across from him.

"I really know very little about it, sir." Jimmy hoped he didn't sound as ignorant as he felt.

"Most people don't. They prefer to leave that to their ministers. But there's a world of wealth in those old tomes. Anytime you would like to borrow one, please feel free to do so."

Excitement gripped Jimmy. "Thank you. That's very generous."

"Nonsense. My offer is purely selfish. I seldom have anyone with whom to discuss my books. It would be a rare treat." He smiled and waved toward the door. "I'm sure the ladies have finished cleaning the kitchen. Cici and Helen won't be happy with me if I keep you here any longer."

Jimmy and Eddy thanked their host and joined the girls. Jimmy hoped to have a few moments of private conversation with Cici, but after a rousing game of croquet, Helen suggested they play checkers. Before they knew it, Mrs. Willow entered the dining room with a platter of sandwiches and fruit. They ate and then headed back to the church for the evening service.

Afterward, Jimmy managed to speak to Cici on the front step of the church. "I enjoyed the day, Cici. You have a wonderful family. Thanks for your hospitality."

A pretty pink blush appeared on her cheeks. "It was my pleasure. Thank you for coming."

"Do you think. . . ?" He cleared his throat. "That is, perhaps I can return the hospitality someday soon and you could have dinner at my sister's home."

"Perhaps." A dimple appeared at one corner of her lips. "I'd have to get permission from my parents."

"Of course."

She offered her hand. He took it and then wasn't quite sure what to do with it. Finally, he gave it a slight shake, bowed, and left.

"You dunce," he berated himself. "She probably expected you to kiss her hand like you did before."

"Hey, Jimmy, wait a minute." Eddy huffed after him, his cheeks red from puffing. "Well," he panted, "seems you decided to ignore my warning about Cici."

Jimmy glared. "I don't know why you don't like her. She's perfectly delightful, and your description of a siren doesn't fit her at all."

Eddy threw his hands in the air. "Okay, buddy. Sorry I said anything. I wish you well."

They headed for the streetcar, where they said good-bye, since they were going in different directions.

Jimmy rode to the elevated train station. On the way home, his mind kept jumping from Cici to the morning sermon. The chance to talk to Rev. Willow about the scripture hadn't arisen, but he determined to speak to the minister about it the first chance he got.

&

Cici sat on the seat of the wobbling streetcar, her back rigid. She'd told her mother she was going to lunch with a friend and rushed out of the house before she could ask for more information. A niggling thought worried her mind. She'd never felt the need to be evasive about her friends before. But somehow she knew her parents wouldn't approve of Gail. Cici took a deep breath and shoved the thought away. After all, she wasn't a child. She was plenty old enough to choose her friends. And there was nothing wrong with Gail. Cici was sure of it.

The streetcar carried her to the downtown district, past department stores and salons. After a few blocks, she pulled the cord and got off. She glanced around, consternation rising in her. The neighborhood was rather rough looking. She bit her bottom lip and wondered if perhaps she should turn around and go home. A surge of fear shot through her, but with it came a thrill of excitement. Her eyes scanned the nearby buildings and came to rest on a sign that proclaimed TONY'S PLACE.

She swallowed and ran her tongue over her dry lips. She'd never felt timid or fearful before and didn't intend to start now. She took a resolute step forward and walked down the street to the café. There, that wasn't so bad. She reached out for the doorknob, but a laughing couple shoved past her and opened the door.

Cici gave an indignant glare to the retreating couple, then stopped inside the door and glanced around. The room sparkled with bright lights, and a small orchestra played merry music in a rear corner. Her nose inhaled the smell of smoke and perfume mingled with the zesty aromas drifting from the kitchen.

"Cici, over here."

She turned.

Gail beckoned from a small round table.

With relief, Cici headed in her direction.

"Hey, I'm so glad you came. Put your coat on the extra chair. They never have enough coatracks here."

Flustered by the daring adventure and Gail's exuberance, Cici sat across from the laughing brunette.

A waitress came with menus and glasses of water.

Cici scanned the selections and the girls placed their orders.

"I wasn't sure you'd come." Gail tossed her a sideways grin.

"Why? I said I'd be here."

"I know. I just thought you might change your mind and back out."

"Well, I almost did when I saw the neighborhood." She glanced around nervously. "Are you sure we're safe here? It doesn't look quite respectable."

"Nonsense. Don't be a baby. Some very interesting people come here. You know. . .show business folks and such."

"Really?" Cici forgot her fears at this exciting news. "Have you ever met any?"

"Sure. All the time. Some of the cast of *The Scarlet Lady* hang around here a lot."

Cici gasped. "What's that? It doesn't sound nice."

"Sure it is. Upper class and all that."

"Well, if you say so." But dread tightened her chest.

"Gail sipped from her water glass. "You look very pretty today. I'm glad to see you painted those lips."

"Yes," Cici whispered, looking around. "Is it noticeable?"

"Of course. It's supposed to be noticed. Why else would you wear it?" She gave a little laugh.

Indignation flooded Cici. Was Gail mocking her?

"Oh dear. That was rude. I'm sorry, Cici. Sarcasm just seems to come naturally to me."

"It's all right. You weren't rude. I tend to be overly sensitive at times."

"Well then, good. We're still friends." Gail reached over

and patted her hand.

Their food arrived and Cici bowed her head and said a silent prayer. She looked up and found Gail staring at her. "What's wrong?" Didn't Gail give thanks for her food?

"Nothing." Gail picked up her hamburger and took a large bite. "Mmm. Don't you love hamburgers?"

"They're all right, I guess." Cici bit a small corner off her ham sandwich and tried not to look at the grease on Gail's mouth. They chatted between bites. Finally, Cici pushed her plate back.

"How about some pie?" Gail looked around for the waitress.

"No, I couldn't eat another bite." She glanced at the watch at the end of her neck chain. "I should probably be going."

"Stay awhile longer. We've hardly had a chance to talk yet."

"Well, maybe a few minutes."

"Gail! Darling! How nice to see you." An older man had stepped to their table and stood smiling at Gail.

The girl flung her head back and looked up with a saucy grin. "Well, Sutton, it's been a long time. Where have you been keeping yourself?"

"I've been directing a show in Paris, my dear. I arrived home last week." He glanced at Cici. "And who is your charming companion?"

"Oh, forgive my bad manners. Cici Willow, I'd like to introduce you to James Sutton, an old family friend." She glanced back at Mr. Sutton. "Cici and I, on the other hand, met only recently, but I believe we're on our way to becoming best pals."

Cici blushed and offered her hand to the gentleman. He lifted it and let his lips linger on her fingers for a moment. Startled, Cici jerked her hand away, heart hammering.

His lips tipped in an amused smile. "Ah. Forgive my clumsiness, my dear. Your beauty quite overcame me for a moment."

"Won't you join us, Sutton?" Gail interrupted. "Tell us about the Paris show?"

"I would be delighted. That is, if your young friend has no objection." He turned his eyes on Cici. Deep, dark eyes that seemed to search her entire being.

What was it about him that fascinated her so? He was as old as her father. And the feelings he elicited in her were certainly not romantic. Yet she found herself wanting to stay in his presence. To hear his deep, soothing voice.

She cleared her throat. "No, I have no objection. I'd love to hear about the show, Mr. Sutton."

five

"But Danni, I love working on the docks and couldn't pass up the opening." He stared down at his weeping sister, helpless at the unusual sight. "It'll be all right."

She wiped her eyes and sniffled. "Jimmy, have you forgotten so soon? How could you enjoy a place that is so wicked and cruel to children? Even before Sutton got us in his clutches, don't you remember how we walked the streets till we were exhausted, then hid on the wharf, cold and starving, even to the point of my stealing someone else's lunch?"

Jimmy patted her shoulder, wondering how to explain. "I do remember, Danni. But for some reason, I feel drawn to the area. I love the excitement of the harbor and the ships that moor there."

"Oh, Jimmy."

"But it's not just that." He walked to the window and glanced out. Late afternoon shadows fell across the opulent green lawn. Like the shadows that had reached out to him in his dreams, bringing him to his latest decision. Should he open up to her? Mention the children whose hungry eyes haunted his dreams and waking hours? Should he tell her of the cries of his heart to help them? "There are the children."

She glanced up, a startled look in her eyes. "Is that what this is about? Have you been helping the children?"

He returned and sat beside her on the settee. "Not much. I'm not sure what I can do besides offer a bite of something now and then. Eddy is the one they flock to. They're drawn to him like a bug to light, but he's only there for an hour and sometimes he can't make it."

She bit her lip. "So it is the children."

"Not just the children. If you could see the hopeless looks on the faces of the mothers. . ."

She laid her hand on his and looked into his eyes. "Please, Jimmy," she whispered, "there are other ways to help these people. You know I'm part of a charitable foundation to help the poor of the city. I'll try to get more people interested in helping out around the wharf area. Go back to school. Don't throw your future away."

He groaned. "Maybe I'm losing my mind, turning my back on a career in the Nelson firm. You and Blake must think I'm completely ungrateful, and I'm not. It's just. . . I don't know, Danni. I'm sorry to make you cry. But I can't leave the docks. At least not yet."

She turned, her face ashen, and walked from the room.

Jimmy hit his fist against the windowsill. *Idiot. Why'd you tell her? Of course she'll worry.*

He took a deep breath. At least he hadn't mentioned Cobb, who'd actually introduced him to the dock supervisor.

It had taken a few days to work out a system where he could help without compromising his job. He'd followed Eddy's lead and made sure he had extra food in his lunch pail, but most days, he gave it all away. He chuckled. Cook must wonder about the enormous quantities of food he stuffed into his lunch pail, as well as the amounts he consumed at breakfast and dinner.

He headed upstairs to get a book from his room. He had intended to join the family for dinner before going to Rev. Willow's for a Bible study, but under the circumstances, it might be best if he left early. Tonight they planned to discuss the topic of salvation by grace. Jimmy had accepted Jesus as his Savior when he was twelve, but in spite of the fact that Danni and Blake had a close relationship with God, Jimmy had never really studied the Bible for himself. The reverend had been teaching him the fundamentals of Christianity, and it had opened up a world of truth and light to him. He couldn't seem to get enough. He couldn't understand the insatiable hunger that seemed to drive him to more and more spiritual understanding; he could only follow it.

The fact that he was thrown more and more into Cici's presence was an added joy and benefit.

✺

"Cici, see who is at the door, please. I think Papa is expecting Mr. Grayson."

"Yes, Mother." Cici laid her book on the table by her chair and went to the door. Why hadn't Papa told her Jimmy was coming? She was supposed to meet Gail and some other friends at Tony's at seven.

"Hello, Jimmy." She opened the screen door and let him in.

"Cici. It's nice to see you." He cleared his throat. "It's such a wonderful evening, I was wondering if you'd like to go for a walk after the Bible study."

Now what should she do? Gail and her crazy gang of friends were so exciting. She couldn't remember when she'd had so much fun. But Jimmy, well, Jimmy made her heart go wild, just as it was doing right now. Why did he have to be so handsome? But she'd had handsome beaux before. So what was it that made Jimmy so special? "Thank you. That would be nice, if it's all right with Papa."

"Would you like for me to ask him?"

"If you'd like. I have to go out for a while, but I'll be back before your meeting is over."

She smiled as Jimmy went to join her father in the study. Of course. The Bible study would last a couple of hours. She could go to the café and be back before then. She breathed a sigh of relief and went into the parlor, where her mother was mending the lace on a collar. "I'll be back soon, Mother."

"Very well, dear. Tell Helen's mother hello for me."

"Yes, ma'am." Guilt tugged at her heart as she kissed her mother and headed for the door. But she hadn't said she was

going to Helen's. Not tonight or the other times she'd gone
out with Gail. So she hadn't lied. Cici stood at the corner
and attempted to brush away the thoughts running through
her head. Maybe she hadn't lied with words, but she was
practicing deception. She breathed a sigh of relief as the
streetcar came rumbling down the street.

The café was thick with smoke. She hadn't noticed it being
this smoky before. She hoped it wouldn't cling to her hair
and clothing.

"What's the matter, Cici girl? Why so glum?" Carl Foster,
one of the young men in her new circle of friends, took her
hand and began to lead her to the long table where the others
waited.

"Don't sit down, you two." Gail jumped up. "We were just
about to head over to the Blue Gardenia. You're just in time,
Cici."

"Oh, but I can't stay long. Couldn't we remain here instead?"
Cici had no idea how far away the Blue Gardenia was.

"There's no action here tonight. Besides, I promised Sutton we'd meet him there. He's recently returned from New
York City."

Cici bit her lip. "But I have to be home by nine. I have
another commitment."

"Don't worry about it. Someone will drive you."

"I would be honored to escort you home in my trusty
flivver whenever you wish to go." Carl bowed, and as he lifted
his head, Cici's nose twitched at the smell of alcohol.

"Flivver?"

Gail snorted. "He means his wreck of an automobile."

Carl frowned. "I resent that. And so does my flivver. And
so do all the girls."

"Thank you, Mr. Foster, but I don't think so."

Gail and several others laughed. "Good choice, Cici. In
another hour, he won't be able to drive anyway. Someone will
take you home. Don't worry about it."

Cici allowed herself to be persuaded. After all, it would be rude to leave so soon. And besides, it would be nice to see the mysterious Mr. Sutton again.

When the party of six divided up between a carriage and Carl's automobile, Cici made sure not to end up in the latter. They rode several blocks, amid boisterous conversation, and pulled up in front of a brightly lit club. The front of the building sported a huge picture of a diamond and the name in large blue letters below.

A shiver of excitement offset the twinge of fear that ran through Cici as they pushed through the door of the club. She had accompanied them to restaurants that served liquor before and a few of them drank a little, but this was the first time she'd been inside an actual nightclub. Cloth-covered tables encircled an empty space where couples danced. The room was nearly dark, the only lights an occasional shaded oil lamp and a few low-burning gaslights spaced on the walls.

A waiter approached and led them to a table toward the rear of the room. As they neared a large round table, James Sutton rose and bowed, motioning them to chairs. Somehow when they were all seated, Cici found herself next to their host with Gail on his other side.

"The delightful Miss Cecilia Willow. How very nice to see you again." He leaned his head toward her and smiled. "I hope you've been well."

Cici swallowed. "Yes, I'm very well, thank you."

"I'm most happy to hear it, my dear." His voice rolled over her like silk, and she felt herself relax. What a nice man. And so charming.

Raucous music blared across the room. Cici started and put her hands to her ears.

"Hey, Cici, c'mon. Let's cut a rug." Carl had jumped up from his chair across the table and stood at her side, his hand extended to her.

"What?"

"Aw, honey, haven't you ever heard of ragtime?" He danced a few strange dance steps where he stood; then he grinned.

"I don't dance, Carl. You'll have to excuse me."

"Don't dance? Of course you do. Everyone dances." His words slurred, and Cici was thankful she wouldn't have to ride home with him.

"Miss Willow doesn't wish to dance, Carl." Sutton's voice was firm and his smile grim, and something in that smile, Cici wasn't sure what, passed between the two men.

"Oh, I see." Carl's face had turned ashen. "I mean, sure. That's fine. I'm sorry, Cici. That is, Miss Willow." He stumbled across to one of the other girls, and the two of them made their way to the dance floor.

Cici sat stunned, not sure what had just happened but glad Carl no longer bothered her.

Sutton turned to her with a smile, quite unlike the one he'd given Carl. "I'm sorry if he annoyed you with his attentions, my dear."

"Thank you. I don't think he meant any harm though."

"You may be right. The young man has had too much to drink." He smiled then turned to Gail. "Now to a more pleasant subject. I would like to extend an invitation to all you young people to accompany me down to my friend John Cowell's lake house for an evening of symphony and excellent dining."

Gail's eyes were bright. "Wonderful. Mr. Cowell always throws a great shindig."

"Yes, well, I think this will be a little more refined than a shindig." His expression had grown stern.

"Sorry. Of course, I meant to say soiree, not shindig." The girl's face flamed.

What was it about Sutton? He could be charming one moment and almost threatening the next. He patted Gail's hand. "Of course you did, my dear." He turned to Cici. "I would be very pleased if you would accompany us. That is, if you're free on Friday night of next week."

"Why, I don't know." Should she?

"We will take a passenger boat from the Clark Street dock, sail downriver, then across the lake to the Cowell mansion."

A mansion? Cici's heart hammered at the enticing idea. But would she dare?

"It's very kind of you to invite me, Mr. Sutton. I'll have to let you know." She stood. "I really must go now."

"Let me find someone to take you, Cici." Gail rose.

"No need for that." Sutton tossed a wad of bills on the table and rose. "I would be honored to drive you both home."

Cici was relieved when he drove her home first. He made no comment when she asked to be let off at the streetcar stop. She hurried down the street to her house and rushed upstairs to her room. She must shed these smoke-saturated clothes before anyone saw her.

⁊⁊

Jimmy offered his arm to Cici and they strolled down the sidewalk. The girl, who had been so quiet earlier, seemed fidgety. "Have I done or said something to offend you?"

"What? I mean, excuse me? What did you say?"

"You seem distracted. I thought perhaps I'd said something to offend you."

She peered up at him. "Oh no. I seem to have a slight headache. That's all."

"Oh. Forgive me." Jimmy stopped and turned to her. "Would you prefer to postpone our walk for another time?"

"No, I think perhaps the fresh air might help." She blushed and Jimmy's heart turned over. What a sweet, precious girl she was. They continued down the sidewalk.

"How is the work on the docks going? Do you still enjoy working there?"

"Yes, but it's difficult to see the poverty-stricken children." He frowned. "There's so much I want to do for them, and so little I can."

"You're very sweet, Jimmy, to want to help them." Her voice had softened. "But there are so many of them. What can one person do?"

"I don't know, Cici. But I have to try. My sister's charity group is going to help. So that's a start."

"Perhaps the church could help, too."

Jimmy looked at her in surprise. This was the first time she'd shown any interest in the conditions of the residents in the dock area. Encouraged, he talked as they strolled along, until finally they arrived back at the parsonage.

They stepped up on the porch and Jimmy glanced at the swing. "Could we sit on the swing for a while and talk?"

"Yes, I'd like that." Her eyes crinkled as she smiled.

Jimmy's heart flopped in his chest. Had there ever been a sweeter, prettier girl? Eddy must be crazy. He and his warnings. Probably jealous.

They leaned back. Would he dare take her hand? Better not.

"Oh, Jimmy, would you look at those stars? I don't think I've ever seen anything so bright and lovely. They about take my breath away." Her lips parted and her eyes widened in delight.

"I have." Uh-oh. He hadn't meant to say that aloud. But since he had, he might as well go ahead. "Your eyes are even brighter and lovelier."

He watched, captivated, as pink washed over her face. Her lips began to tilt and she straightened them, pressing them firmly together.

"I hope I haven't offended you, Cici."

She faced him, and this time her lips curved in a sweet smile. "Only if you didn't mean it."

A bubble of pleasure swelled his chest and he laughed. "I assure you I meant it."

"In that case, thank you very much." She rose and tossed him a saucy grin. "And now, I believe it's time for me to say good night."

He stood. "Must you?"

"Yes, I must. Good night, Jimmy." She slipped inside and the door shut softly behind her.

Jimmy stood for several moments, unable to stop the idiotic grin he knew was on his face. He walked to the street-car stop, his heart light. What an evening. The Bible study had been enlightening and uplifting. And to top it off, a stroll around the block and a private conversation, albeit very short, with the sweetest girl in the world. And the most delightful good night he'd ever known.

six

The dock teemed with activity. Almost as much as in the daylight hours. Stevedores yelled at each other in their haste to get cargo loaded and stacked. But most of the action came from passengers waiting to board the two huge ships hugging the harbor.

Jimmy stretched his aching back and wiped a sleeve across his forehead. In spite of the cold late April wind blowing off the water, he'd worked up a river of perspiration. He'd been glad of the extra hours when Stephen had asked him to cover his shift. But fourteen hours of hauling heavy crates and boxes was taking its toll on him. He slipped his watch from his pocket. Eight o'clock. His shift wouldn't end till two. He sighed. He'd make it though.

"Hey, Jimbo. Here's the last one." Cobb hauled a heavy crate over the deck and Jimmy grabbed one end. Together they maneuvered it down the stairs to the galley supply area and battened it down.

"Whew! What's in that one anyway?" They'd all been heavy, but that one was a doozy.

"Wine for miladies and gents." Cobb gave a mocking bow and laughed. "C'mon, let's go eat some supper."

They grabbed their tin pails from the dockworkers' shack and headed for a couple of upturned crates at the other side of the dock. Jimmy had learned, these last two weeks, that if he stayed too close to the loading area, his break was likely to be cut short by someone needing a hand.

Cobb opened his pail and retrieved a hunk of cheese and a piece of bread. "I don't get you, Jimbo."

"What do you mean?"

44

"Well, I know why I'm breaking my back with all the extra work I can get. But why are you down here at night when you could be having fun with your little clean-cut pals?"

"You don't think I need to earn money?" Ignoring the remark about his other friends, Jimmy pried the lid off his bucket and looked at Cobb.

"Not like I do, old boy." Cobb spoke around an enormous bite of cheese. "I mean, you live with Danni and that rich lawyer husband of hers. It ain't like you have to earn a living."

"Believe it or not, my friend, I don't wish to be dependent on my brother-in-law forever. I figure it's high time I start earning my own way."

"Prob'ly shoulda stayed in law school, then, buddy. You'd get there a lot faster."

Jimmy pulled a cloth-wrapped sandwich from his pail, his mouth watering at the smell of ham and cheese.

A faint cough drew his attention. Two small boys stood at the top of the steps leading up to the dock, their eyes wide, watching Cobb as he crammed another hunk of cheese in his mouth. The Daly boys, six-year-old Patrick and his little brother, Mike, who wasn't more than three. A little late for them to venture out.

Jimmy smiled and crooked his finger, motioning them over.

They grinned and broke out in a run, stopping in front of him.

"I wonder if you boys could help me out here." Jimmy pursed his lips and gave them a very serious look. "You see, my sister loaded my lunch bucket down with so much food I'll never be able to eat it. It'd be a shame to throw this good stuff away. But if I take it back home, she might think I don't like it."

Both boys nodded their heads, causing their filthy blond curls to bounce.

Jimmy shook his head. "I'd sure hate to hurt her feelings like that."

More nods. This time eager, hopeful nods.

"Do you think you could help me out here and eat some of it for me?"

"Yes, sir." Little Mike's excited voice tugged at Jimmy's heart.

Cobb snorted.

"Yeah, we wouldn't want your sister's feelin's to be hurt or anything." Patrick ran his tongue across his cracked lips.

Jimmy tore a sandwich in half and gave an exaggerated sigh of relief. "Well, I sure do thank you both. Here. See if you can take care of this for me."

Their red, chapped little fingers clutched at the food he handed them.

"Now, don't gobble it down too fast. I wouldn't want you to get a stomachache when you're only trying to help me out."

They took small bites and chewed slowly. Still, the sandwiches were gone all too soon. Jimmy reached inside his bucket and produced a banana. He divided it and handed the two pieces over to Patrick and Mike.

When they'd finished, he took some coins from his pocket and handed them to Patrick. "Would you take this to Bridget and tell her to buy food?"

"Yes, sir. Thank you, sir." Patrick crammed the coins into his pocket and grabbed Mike by the hand. They ran down the steps and toward the tenement-lined street.

Jimmy winced as he saw the soles of their shoes flopping loose against the dirt street.

"Okay. I take back everything I said. I see now where yer money's going." Cobb shook his head. "Jimbo, Jimbo. When are you gonna stop trying to save the world? Look out for yourself. That's what I always say."

"The boys are orphans. Their sister is raising them."

Cobb shrugged, took an apple out of his bucket, and wiped it on his dingy pant leg. "So what? Some kids don't have a sister to look out for them." He grinned. "Maybe it's the sister you're interested in?"

"Bridget is ten years old."

Cobb's hand stopped in midair, halfway to his mouth. He dropped his arm and stood. "Let's get back to work." He laid the apple on the box and headed toward the loading area.

Jimmy pushed the bucket lid down and got up. Halfway across the dock, he stopped still, his heart thumping fast. What was she. . .

Cici had just stepped on the gangplank of the *Lady Fair*. She seemed to be part of a group of several young people. A young man put his hand on her shoulder. She shrugged it off. The girl beside her leaned over and said something. Cici laughed and turned her head, her eyes staring straight into Jimmy's. She froze, her eyes rounding and her rosebud mouth dropping open.

Jimmy nodded.

She clamped her mouth shut and gave a little wave, then hurried up the gangplank after her companions.

Why was Cici boarding a tour boat this time of night? And who were the people she was with? They certainly weren't members of their church. Was she in some kind of trouble? Should he go after her? But she had seemed to know the young man and woman.

"Hey, Jimbo, you coming? We gotta load the *Monarch*." Cobb, waving both hands, stood on the deck of the cargo ship.

"Coming." He scanned the deck of the *Lady Fair* but saw no sign of Cici. He was more than likely making a mountain out of a molehill, as the saying went. Surely her parents wouldn't have allowed her to go off on a boat with people they didn't know and approve of. Laughing at his own imagination, he hurried up the *Monarch*'s gangplank.

❧

Silver tinkled against crystal, drawing Cici from her reverie. They had seated her next to Sutton who sat on the host's left. Gail sat across from her next to an older man who'd been introduced as Mr. Cowell's brother, William.

Cici smiled at the tall, thin waiter who had just placed a generous slice of chocolate cake, covered in some kind of sauce, in front of her. He nodded and stepped over to serve Carl.

When he moved away, Carl turned to her. "Hey, this is real Haviland china. Don'tcha think?"

Cici nodded and took a small bite of the rich concoction. What terrible luck that Jimmy had been working tonight. What must he think? She swallowed and took a deep breath. If her parents found out. . . Well, that simply could not happen. She must get to Jimmy and ask him not to say anything around them. She'd have to try to think up some reason. Her heart sank. Up to now, she'd managed to keep seeing her new companions and still avoid outright lying. It might not be possible this time. How had she gotten herself into this situation? Why was she hanging out with such a worldly group of people anyway?

Sutton's smooth voice invaded her thoughts. "Have you enjoyed your dinner, my dear?"

She forced herself to smile. "Yes, thank you. Very much."

"I believe everyone is about to retire to the drawing room. I must speak privately to our host, but I'll join you shortly. It's only a business matter that will not keep me for long." He rose, bowed, and followed Mr. Cowell out of the room.

Several of the guests departed, leaving Cici and Gail and their group alone. A servant entered the room and asked them to follow him.

The drawing room turned out not to be a drawing room at all, but some sort of gaming area. Tables were positioned around the room. Each held decks of cards, dice, and other objects. Cici felt suddenly faint. Two of the tables were already occupied by men and women who'd apparently been there for some time. Glasses containing what Cici was sure was liquor rested next to them.

"Hey, what's wrong? You're white as a ghost." Gail stood by her side, a frown on her face.

"Gail, those people are gambling." Her voice had risen, but at the moment, she didn't care.

"Of course they are, silly. What's wrong with that?" Lines appeared between her eyes. "Don't tell me you're going to make a fuss because of some old-fashioned sense of guilt. Everyone gambles nowadays, Cici. Even refined folks like the Cowells."

"I. . .I hadn't intended to make a fuss, of course. I'm simply not sure I should stay."

Gail huffed. "Cici, you have no choice. The boat won't be leaving for at least two more hours. If you don't wish to play, you don't have to. As you can see, there are sofas and chairs by the fireplace. You can sit there. Chances are, someone will join you, so you won't have to sit alone all evening."

"Couldn't you sit with me?" She shouldn't have said that. It sounded immature even to her own ears. "Never mind. I'll be fine."

She found a magazine and sat on the edge of a chair that turned out to be hard and uncomfortable.

If only she had stayed home tonight. Her parents thought she was spending the night at Helen's when she actually planned to stay at Gail's. Cici sincerely hoped the girl wouldn't drink much.

She took a deep breath and her heart fluttered. She didn't belong here. Her parents had taught her better. Why couldn't she be faithful to God and her upbringing? The night she and Jimmy had sat on the porch and looked at the stars had been so sweet, so innocent. She really thought she might be falling in love with him a little. So what was wrong with her? Why had she come with these people?

As the evening dragged on, the room filled with smoke from cigars and cigarettes. Cici slipped out the French doors and sat on a cushioned wrought iron bench. She shivered as the cold wind off the lake swept over her, wishing she'd slipped her wrap on. But anything was better than the stuffy drawing room. Stars flashed and twinkled in the dark night sky, reflecting on the surface of the lake. She leaned back and wrapped her arms around her shoulders.

"So there you are. I thought perhaps I'd find you here." Sutton's tall form appeared in the doorway, her wrap over one arm. He stepped through and shut the doors behind him. "I was getting concerned."

"I needed a breath of fresh air." She thanked him as he slipped the stole around her shoulders.

"Of course you did. The drawing room has become abominable. I think we must leave soon."

Cici didn't answer, but waves of relief washed over her. She'd thought the night would never end.

"I hope you aren't offended by the card playing. I know your father is a minister."

Cici started. "I'm surprised you're aware of that. I don't believe I've told anyone." In fact, she was almost certain she hadn't.

"Perhaps you've forgotten. I believe Gail mentioned it." He sat next to her and leaned back, his shoulder pressing against hers. Uncomfortable, she moved, leaning as close to the end of the bench as she could.

He shifted and straightened.

She shrugged. Perhaps she had forgotten as he suggested.

The *Lady Fair* pulled into the Clark Street dock after midnight. Tired and disturbed about the evening, Cici wished she could go home. But what would she tell her parents? Having no other recourse, she got into a carriage with Gail and went home with her as planned. Cici almost gagged in the enclosed space at the smell of liquor on Gail's breath. As they climbed the stairs to Gail's apartment, the girl stumbled and cursed.

Later, Cici lay on her side on a narrow cot in Gail's bedroom.

Drunken snores rumbled throughout the room. Suddenly Gail didn't seem so exciting. She only seemed pathetic.

æ

Disbelief clouded Jimmy's mind. Surely Cici wasn't asking him to keep secrets from her parents. As he stared at her, a pink blush tinged her cheeks.

He'd been about to walk into the church for the morning service when she'd appeared as though out of nowhere, in a sky blue dress that brought out the deep azure of her eyes, and asked to speak to him. His heart had beat double time, eagerly awaiting her words. But never would he have expected this.

"Oh dear. I know you must think I'm horrid, Jimmy. You see, I spent the night with Helen and forgot to tell Papa and Mama we were visiting friends upriver. Please don't misunderstand."

"But Cici, don't you think you should simply explain to them?" Confusion clouded his mind.

"But you see, they worry so. And if they knew I went somewhere without their knowing, they'd worry themselves sick about what might have happened." She bit her lip and sent him a pleading look. "And I'm not asking you to lie about anything. Just don't mention it unless the matter should come up."

Okay, that really made things clear. Surely the Willows would want to know about this. But it wasn't his place to tell them unless they asked, and that wasn't likely.

"Please, Jimmy. Papa has so much on his mind. And Mama had heart palpitations a few days ago. She said it was nothing, but I can't help but be concerned."

He inhaled deeply.

Tears had formed in Cici's eyes and she blinked hard to hold them back. She must be very worried about her mother. And what if she was right? What if he told them and Mrs. Willow had a heart attack or brain seizure?

"All right, Cici. I think you're making a mistake, but an honest mistake, so I'll honor your request. I doubt there would be an occasion for the subject to come up anyway." Jimmy's heart raced at the relief that swept over her face.

"Oh, Jimmy, thank you so much. I promise I'll never forget to tell them where I'm going again."

His heart jumped as she reached a hand out and placed it on his cheek. Of course, there was nothing wrong with what she asked. She'd simply made a mistake and was concerned about how it would affect her parents. Totally reasonable. He reached up and took her hand in his.

seven

"I've taught you all the basics, Jimmy, and you've learned well. Your hunger for knowledge of the Word amazes and thrills me."

Warmth flowed through Jimmy at Rev. Willow's words of praise.

"Thank you, sir. I don't know how to thank you for all your help. I thought I knew the basics of Christianity but discovered I knew very little. I'm sorry to see our studies end."

"Actually, Jimmy, they needn't end. I plan to begin a series of in-depth Bible studies starting next Tuesday night at the church. If you're interested, you're welcome to join us."

"I'm very interested." Jimmy couldn't believe it. There was so much he wanted to know, and he felt totally unready to start out on his own. Sometimes the Bible seemed like a great mystery that he'd never understand. But he'd learned the past few weeks that God wanted to reveal those mysteries to His children.

"Good. Then be at the church at seven. We have a number of people signed up. I believe you'll find a group study very beneficial."

"I'm sure I will, sir." He shook the reverend's hand and left the study. Disappointed not to see Cici, he stepped out onto the porch. Moonlight washed over her and the wicker porch swing.

"Hi, Jimmy." She smiled and patted the seat next to her. "So this was your last study, wasn't it?"

He leaned back in the seat beside her. "Yes, I was feeling

rather lost about that. But then your father told me about the new Tuesday study at the church."

"You're not going to join?" Wrinkles appeared between her eyes and disappointment filled her voice.

Confused, he stared at her. "Well, yes, I thought I would. Why?"

"We hardly see each other at all, Jimmy. Sundays at both services and sometimes Sunday afternoons for dinner. I'd hoped perhaps you would save that time slot for me." She blushed and turned away. "Forgive me for being so forward. Perhaps I've misunderstood. I thought you'd want to spend more time with me."

"Not at all. I mean you haven't misunderstood. I want nothing more than to spend time with you." Puzzled, he peered at her. "There are other evenings, Cici. What does one thing have to do with the other?"

Cici bit her lip. "You're right. I don't know what I was thinking." She stood. "I really must go inside. I'm not feeling well. Good night, Jimmy."

Jimmy stared after her then headed down to catch the streetcar. Now what was that about? If she liked him, as she'd implied, he'd have thought she would want him to learn as much about the Bible as he could and grow spiritually. After all, she was a minister's daughter.

⁂

"What's wrong with you today, Grayson? Get a move on."

Jimmy looked up to see the first mate of the *Heron* leaning over the rail and shaking his fist.

"Sorry, I'm coming." He couldn't really blame the man for yelling at him. He'd had Cici and her strange behavior on his mind all morning and had probably been dragging his heels. He practically ran up the gangplank and went to help a couple of stevedores stack crates to make room for more.

"Okay, Grayson, get back dockside and bring another one up. Go help him, McDugan. These crates are heavy."

Jimmy started down the gangplank when a figure down below caught his eye. A chill ran through him. The man's tall stature, the set of his shoulders, and the way he sauntered across the dock were all too familiar.

Jimmy frowned. No, it couldn't be Sutton. He had two more years to serve. They'd said he wouldn't be eligible for early release. But it sure looked like. . .

The man turned.

Jimmy clamped his teeth together. Anger rose like bile inside him. It was Sutton. Jimmy watched as the man who'd exploited him and Danni and many other children strolled down the side street parallel to the bridge as though he hadn't a care. The same street Danni and Jimmy had raced down with an angry dockworker in pursuit. And there was the alley where Cobb grabbed them and jerked them out of sight. Sutton was headed to the run-down house where he'd operated his child crime ring.

Another stab of anger pierced him. Would the man be stupid enough to have another gang of children stealing for him? Surely not. The authorities must be keeping an eye on him.

"Hey, Grayson. What you standin' there for? I ain't loading this doozy by myself."

Sutton had moved on down the street, out of sight.

Jimmy joined McDugan and went back to work. When he broke for the midday meal, he headed for the part of the dock next to the street. Craning his neck, he looked as far as he could see, but no sign of Sutton remained.

"Jimbo, what you gazing at?" Cobb joined him, his lunch pail swinging from his hand.

"You won't believe it. I just saw Sutton."

A shadow crossed Cobb's eyes, but he didn't reply as he sat on a crate and opened his bucket.

"Did you hear what I said? I saw Sutton walking down the street toward the old place."

"Aw, you must have been seein' things, Jimbo. Sutton's

locked up. He ain't around here."

"No, it was him. I wasn't sure at first. Then he turned and I saw his face." Jimmy sat but didn't move to open his lunch pail. "It was him all right."

"Hmm. I'll ask around. But I think you're imagining it, old man." Cobb laughed, but his laugh was shaky. "You were just a kid last time you saw him. Easy to make a mistake. You probably wouldn't even recognize him if you saw him now."

Jimmy stared at his friend. Why was he so sure it wasn't Sutton? Or maybe he knew it was. Could Cobb be involved with Sutton again? After all the trouble he'd caused him? Jimmy hoped not. He and Cobb had always been friends, but even more so in the last few months. He'd hate to see him get into trouble again.

He ate in silence. What should his first move be? He needed to tell Blake right away. That much went without saying. Sutton might be after Danni. He'd threatened her once before. She could be in danger.

꒰ꔷ꒱

Cici laughed as Jimmy and Eddy chased the soccer ball around the back lawn. May had brought long-awaited springlike weather, and the young people had decided to take advantage of it.

Helen leaned back in her lawn chair and yawned. "It's nice to see the boys having some fun for a change. Jimmy's been so serious lately."

"What's wrong with that, I'd like to know?" Cici had thought the same thing many times and had no idea why Helen's words had brought on the defensive response.

"Why, nothing, I suppose. I wasn't criticizing him."

"I know, I know." Cici frowned and studied Jimmy as he dodged the ball that had flown by his head. "I've no idea what they think they're playing."

Helen giggled. "Me either. Guess they're making up their own game."

"Jimmy *is* rather serious lately. He spends as much time with Papa as he does with me." She bit her lip and cast a sideways glance at Helen.

"Hmm. That's odd." She thought for a moment then sat straight, her eyes wide. "Cici, you don't think. . ." She flopped back against the chair. "Nah. That couldn't be it."

"What couldn't be it?" Cici frowned.

"I just wondered if maybe Jimmy was thinking about the ministry."

"Thinking what about the ministry?" What in the world was she getting at? A chill ran across Cici's skin. "No. No, Helen. Jimmy is going back to law school. I'm sure. This manual labor thing is just a phase he's going through." She laughed, but the sound was unconvincing, even to herself. "He would have told me if he had anything like that in mind."

"Maybe he doesn't know."

"Well, don't you dare say anything."

ès

Jimmy and Cici sat on the porch swing and watched as Eddy and Helen walked toward the streetcar hand in hand.

Cici took a deep breath. "Jimmy, have you decided whether you're going back to law school or not?"

He frowned and shook his head. "I know I need to make a decision soon." He reached over and took her hand, rubbing his thumb over the smooth skin.

Cici shivered but left her hand in his. She ran her tongue over her lips. "Of course, it's none of my business. I shouldn't have asked."

He smiled. "Cici, I hope you will consider my business yours. I care a great deal for you and your opinion."

She inhaled deeply. She cared about Jimmy, too. But how much did they really know about each other? Obviously, there was way too much he didn't know about her. And lately he'd been way too religious. Could Helen possibly be right?

❧

Jimmy stepped onto the streetcar and sat on a slatted seat near the front. Cici's face appeared in his mind as it tended to do when he was quiet. They had been spending a couple of evenings a week together. They'd had some nice long talks and had grown closer. But something seemed to be on her mind. Was she growing tired of him?

He groaned. As if he didn't have enough on his mind. It had been a week since his glimpse of Sutton. Blake had made a phone call and confirmed that Sutton had been released early. The prison was overcrowded and his good behavior had precipitated the decision. Yeah, good behavior. Sutton knew how to manipulate, all right.

Jimmy's mouth tightened as he recalled the fear that slid across Danni's face when they told her. She'd readily agreed not to leave the house without her husband for the present.

If Danni didn't have so much to worry about, he'd talk to her about Cici. Or maybe it would be good for her to get her mind off Sutton for a little while.

❧

"Why must he be so religious?" Cici stepped into Tony's Place with Gail close beside her. "I mean, it's one thing to go to church. Of course I want him to do that. I wouldn't dream of missing a Sunday service myself."

Gail seated herself at their usual table and waited for Cici to sit across from her. She patted a yawn with the back of her hand. "I don't know what your problem is. Why don't you just break up with the guy?"

"What?" The possibility of breaking up with Jimmy had never crossed Cici's mind. The thought of it sent a chill over her. "How can you say that? You know how much I care about him."

Gail gave a little laugh. "If you say so. But I could point out plenty of fellows who'd love to step in and take his place."

Shaking her head, Cici turned to the waiter who'd come to take their order. "Just a cup of tea, please."

Gail ordered coffee, and when the waiter had left, she leaned forward on her elbows. "To be quite honest, my dear, I think you're something of a hypocrite."

Shock bolted through Cici and heat flooded her face. "Excuse me?"

Gail laughed and leaned back in her chair. "You don't need to act so indignant. You're too good for the likes of Carl, who'd give his eyeteeth for one of your smiles. But on the other hand, you think Jimmy is a little too honorable and dull."

"I never said any such thing." Cici frowned. "I merely said he was spending too much time with Papa, studying the Bible."

"Oh well. It doesn't matter to me. If you can get by with living in two worlds, more power to you." She smiled. "Personally, I wouldn't want anything to do with the religious life."

"But Gail, you believe in God, don't you?"

A shadow slid across Gail's eyes and she shrugged. "Used to. Not so much anymore."

"But why?" Cici stared across at her friend.

"It doesn't matter. Now, see? That's what I mean about you being a hypocrite. You're doing everything you can to get away from the religious life, but you're trying to push it on me." She clamped her lips shut as the waiter came with their drinks.

Cici reeled from the words Gail had thrown at her. Was she a hypocrite? She didn't mean to be. She simply wanted to have fun. But she still loved God. At least, she thought she did.

A sick feeling clutched at her stomach and she took a sip of the steaming tea. Was she changing? For the worse? She looked across at Gail. She'd never met anyone who didn't believe in God. Maybe that was the reason for their friendship. Perhaps she was supposed to help Gail regain her faith. Yes, that must be it. This was all part of God's plan.

eight

"Jimmy Grayson!" Danni stood, hands on her hips, staring daggers at him. "Do you mean to tell me you've been seeing a girl for three months and didn't tell me?"

Uh-oh. Jimmy hadn't expected this. Danni had been trying to pair him up with girls for ages. She should be shouting for joy. "Well, I met her about that long ago. We've only been seeing each other for a few weeks. Sorry, Danni. I didn't think about telling you."

Laughter burst from Danni's lips, and she threw her arms around him and hugged him. "I was only teasing. I'm not mad. I'm very, very happy for you."

Jimmy grinned and returned the hug. "Whew. You had me going there for a minute."

"Sorry, little brother. You should have seen the look on your face." Her tinkling laughter filled the room. "So her name is Cecilia Willow?"

"Yes, but everyone calls her Cici."

"What a sweet name. And I'm sure she's just as sweet."

"Yes, she is, sis. I can't wait for you to meet her." Should he tell Danni about the way Cici had been acting lately? Maybe not. He was probably exaggerating the problem.

"Well, we're planning a family picnic a week from Saturday. Why don't you ask her to come so we can meet her?" She pursed her lips and tapped a finger against her cheek. "Blake's parents will be there. And Pops. And the Kramers."

The Kramer family had taken Danielle under their wing when she was trying to get away from Sutton. And they'd taken Jimmy in just as readily. They'd been like family ever since.

"Sounds like a good idea. I'll ask her right away."

She bit her lip. "I hope Pops will behave himself."

Jimmy snickered. "He just likes to have fun. He'll be okay."

"Well, you know how he gets when he starts talking about his vaudeville days."

He bent over and kissed her on the cheek. "You worry too much. Cici will love him."

She smiled. "I know. Do you want to invite some of your friends? She might feel more comfortable with people she knows there."

"Hmm. Not this time. Just Cici." He grinned. "You're a great sister. I don't deserve you."

"I know." She smiled and patted his cheek. "I don't deserve you either."

"And neither of you deserve me." Blake stepped out of the library, laughing, and put his arm around Danni's shoulders. "Now what's going on?"

"Jimmy has a girlfriend, a minister's daughter. Her name is Cici, and Jimmy's going to invite her to the family picnic." She gave an excited giggle.

Jimmy and Blake exchanged amused glances.

"Well now, I don't know if you could say she's my girlfriend. We haven't even seen each other except at church and the parsonage." Jimmy frowned. Maybe Cici wouldn't like being called his girlfriend.

"Well, she's a girl and your friend, right?" Blake grinned and slapped him on the back. "What's her father's name?"

"Rev. Willow. He's the pastor of the Hope of Heaven Community Church."

"Oh yes. I've met him. I understand he's a fine man. Very well respected in the community."

"He is a fine man. And a great teacher. You should come and hear him some Sunday."

"We might just do that."

A maid appeared in the doorway. "Dinner is served."

"Thanks, Marie. We'll be right in." Blake smiled at the girl and she nodded and left.

As Jimmy followed Blake and Danni to the dining room, a picture of Sutton crossed his mind for the first time that evening. He prayed Danni's thoughts wouldn't go there. She appeared more relaxed than she'd been since she first found out Sutton had been released.

The next morning he stepped off the streetcar at the end of the Clark Street Bridge and onto the dock. He spotted Cobb just arriving also. He carried his duffel.

"Hi, Cobb. You shipping out?"

"Yeah. *Eastland*'s leaving on a three-day tour. Can't get along without their head cook." He grinned.

Cobb still denied having seen Sutton, although Jimmy had told him the man was out of prison. It was hard to believe he hadn't run into the man by now if Sutton was hanging out in the area. But then, Jimmy hadn't seen him again either, so maybe he'd only been in the neighborhood to see someone that day. Jimmy wanted to believe his friend was being honest.

"Yeah, I guess not." He grinned. "Don't give them ptomaine poisoning."

"I'll try not to." Cobb waved and headed for the *Eastland*. Passengers were already standing in line to board the big tour boat.

The *Lady Fair* was docked nearby. Jimmy scanned the deck then shook his head. Why did he watch for Cici every time he saw that boat? She'd only been visiting a friend the day she'd boarded the *Lady Fair*.

The morning passed in a hurry and Jimmy headed for his usual spot, lunch in hand. He'd just sat down and opened his pail when Bridget and the boys stepped onto the dock. "Hey, come on over." Jimmy motioned to them. "Glad to see you."

"Hi, Jimmy." Bridget's voice was strong. She grabbed Mike as he started to walk away. "No, Mikey. You stay right by my side. You're not going to get lost again."

"He got lost?" A vise of fear clutched at Jimmy's heart. A tiny boy alone in this neighborhood could get hurt bad.

"Yes, he got away from Patrick. Mrs. Baker found him and brought him home." Her voice didn't falter on the word *home*, although Jimmy knew that home was a discarded, three-sided booth someone had once used to sell vegetables. Somehow, Bridget managed to make a home for them there.

"Did you get the blankets I left at your place?"

"Yes, sir. I thought they must be from you. I had to leave to find food for breakfast."

Jimmy reached in and removed two sandwiches from his pail. He tore one in half and handed the halves to the boys, then held the other sandwich out to Bridget.

She put her hands behind her back and shook her head. "No, sir, I don't need anything for myself. I know you've been feeding my brothers and I didn't want them coming out alone after Mikey getting lost."

Jimmy's eyes burned as he blinked back tears. "Bridget, honey, I'd be honored if you'd share my lunch."

She shook her head, but hunger screamed from her eyes as they darted to the sandwich.

"Do you like stories, Bridget?"

Startled, she turned her eyes from the ham and cheese that stuck out between the slices of bread. "I guess so. Haven't heard any since Ma died."

"Well, I'll tell you what. I'm going to be telling stories to some children this weekend, and I'd appreciate it if you'd let me practice on you so I won't make a fool of myself."

"Oh sure. I don't mind."

"Good." He glanced at the sandwich in his hand. "Well, here, I've already unwrapped this and I can't eat and talk at the same time, so why don't you have it, and when I finish my story, I'll eat the one still in my pail."

She nodded and her little pink tongue darted out and

licked her lips as she accepted the food.

Jimmy stretched the story of Jesus feeding the five thousand as long as possible, dividing the other sandwich and a large piece of cake between the three children.

When they turned to leave, little Mike stopped and ran back to Jimmy. "Are you Jesus?"

"Oh no, Mike. I'm Jimmy, remember?"

"But he's like Jesus, Mikey." Bridget smiled and took the little boy's hand and led him away.

❧

Cici rocked back and forth in the wicker rocker on Helen's front porch. She felt like she'd explode if she didn't tell Helen right now. She grinned at her friend.

Helen laughed and, leaning over, put her hand on the rocker's arm to slow it down. "Cici, you're going to fly right out of that chair if you don't calm down."

"I feel like I'm flying, Helen. He's asked me to join his family for a picnic."

"Yes, you said that a number of times. I think I've got the idea. And what if he did? He's had dinner with your family many times."

"That's not the same, and you know it." She shook her finger at Helen, who grabbed it and pushed it away.

"No, I suppose it's not the same. Men don't usually ask you to meet their families unless they care for you a great deal."

"Exactly." Cici nodded and rocked the chair again.

"But of course you must have known anyway. Else you wouldn't have been sneaking off with him." She shook her head. "What I can't understand is why you found it necessary. Your parents like Jimmy. They wouldn't have objected to his taking you on a date."

Cici stared, confused. "What are you talking about? Jimmy and I haven't been sneaking around."

"Oh, come now, Cici. You might have let me in on it though. I had to do some fast thinking when your mother asked me if we had fun the night you slept over." She smiled. "Now, I know you two didn't spend the night alone, so where were you and with whom?"

Cici swallowed. Oh no. How stupid she was. Why didn't she think about the possibility of her mother saying something to Helen? Her mind darted here and there in an attempt to come up with something. If this got back to Jimmy. . . There was only one thing to do. "Oh, Helen."

"What? What's wrong? You're white as a ghost."

"Helen, I have to tell you something. But you have to promise not to tell anyone."

"Well, of course. You know I wouldn't tell a secret." A worried look crossed her face. "Cici, you're scaring me. What's wrong?"

Cici attempted to swallow but her throat tightened. She forced herself to relax. When she managed to speak, her words were only a whisper. "I wasn't with Jimmy that night."

"Then where. . .who?"

"Let's go for a walk. I don't want your mother or sister to hear."

As Cici bared her soul to Helen, she experienced a freedom she hadn't had since she'd first met Gail and begun her journey of dishonesty. Why had she ever thought a life of worldliness and deceit was exciting? All it had brought her were fear and guilt.

"Oh, Cici, why didn't you tell me?"

"I was too ashamed. I felt as though I was betraying our friendship. And. . .well, I'll admit, I was afraid you'd tell my parents." She darted a questioning look at Helen. "Would you have?"

"I don't know, Cici. I might have." Her brow furrowed and she peered into Cici's eyes. "Have you stopped seeing those people?"

"Well, it's been a couple of weeks. And I've decided not to meet them again."

"I hope you mean it."

Heat seared her face at the accusation. Then pain shot through her. What had she become that her best friend couldn't trust her? She sighed. "Yes, I mean it. But to be honest, I don't know if I can stick to it."

"Cici, I'm sorry, but I don't understand. Just don't do it anymore. It's that simple."

"It's not that easy, Helen. I feel like I'm being pulled in two directions." She blinked back tears as they arrived back in front of Helen's house. "I have to go."

"No, Cici, don't leave mad. I'm sorry."

"I'm not mad. Pray for me, Helen." She hurriedly walked away and headed for the streetcar stop. Fear gripped her, clutching and clawing. What kind of horrible person was she? She knew the scriptures. *"Resist the devil, and he will flee from you."* So why was the temptation still there?

As she tossed and turned in her bed that night, fear rose again. She never should have told Helen. She'd probably lose her friendship. Her breath came in sobs.

Then she stopped and took a deep breath. Wait. She had almost forgotten. Hadn't God arranged her friendship with Gail so that Cici could help her spiritually? Yes, she couldn't desert Gail. This was a thing from God.

But what if Helen decided to get even and tell her parents? Guilt bit at her conscience. Helen wasn't like that. Once more, tears fell, soaking her pillow. She tossed it aside and slid another under her head.

Finally, in the wee hours of the morning, she fell into a fitful sleep.

nine

Michael O'Shannon, the old man Jimmy called Pops, laid his chicken leg on the plate and turned to Cici, pointing his thumb in Jimmy's direction. "Well, lass, and what would you be seeing in this young rapscallion?"

Rapscallion? Jimmy? Cici choked back a laugh. "Well, my papa says he's a fine young man. So it must be so."

"Ah, and it's honoring your father's views, you are. That's a good girl. And your father is absolutely right." He patted her hand then lifted a forkful of potato salad. "You'd best be eating now. You could use a little meat on those bones."

"Papa!" Blake's mother pressed her lips together and threw her father a warning look.

"Don't be twitching your nose at me, Katie O'Shannon." He took a bite from the drumstick.

"Nelson, Papa. Nelson."

"Ah, so it is, Katie girl, and well I know it."

Cici laid her napkin next to her plate and glanced around the long table. Blake and Jimmy had set it up on the lush green expanse of the senior Nelsons' front lawn. Two apple trees blossomed nearby. She closed her eyes for a moment, inhaling the fragrance.

"Lovely here, isn't it? I never get used to it."

Cici opened her eyes. Danielle stood next to her, a pitcher of lemonade in her hand.

"Yes, it's very n–nice," Cici stammered, suddenly shy around this sister whom Jimmy adored so.

"Would you like more lemonade?" Danielle motioned with the pitcher toward Cici's glass.

"Oh yes, thank you." She held the glass steady while Danielle poured.

"I hope we'll have a chance to visit before you go home."

Danielle's sincere smile wrapped Cici like a warm shawl, and she relaxed. "Yes, I'd like that very much." She took a deep breath and smiled at Mr. O'Shannon, who winked at her. Jimmy had told her he used to be onstage, and she hoped the subject would come up. She'd never actually met an actor before.

When the meal was over, Cici followed the ladies over to a group of lawn chairs the men had brought out. She watched, amused, as Jimmy, Blake, his father and grandfather, and the Kramers' fifteen-year-old twin boys laughed and argued while they tossed horseshoes until their arms grew numb. Finally, tired of the game, they joined the ladies.

The twins threw themselves onto the ground, and Jimmy flopped down on the chair next to Cici. "Whew." He winked at Cici and her heart fluttered double time.

"Uh-huh," Mr. O'Shannon cackled. "You lads can't keep up with the men, now, can you?"

Cici grinned. The older man was huffing and puffing, but she was pretty sure no one would mention it.

"Yeah, Pops. Guess you're right." Jimmy grinned and Pops smiled back.

Warmth swept over Cici. Obviously the two had a lot of affection for each other.

"Hey, Pops." Jimmy peered around Cici. "I think Cici would like to hear about your acting days."

The old man's eyes widened and sparkled. "Ah, she would, would she?"

Cici heard a groan and giggled when Blake's mother shook her head and frowned at Jimmy.

"Yes, Mr. O'Shannon, I'm dying to hear all about it." Cici leaned forward.

"Well now, on one condition." He gave her a mock stern look. "There'll be none of this mister stuff. You'll be calling me Pops the same as all the other young folks do."

"Yes, sir. Pops it is." She grinned. He must have been quite a charmer in his heyday.

He coughed and cleared his throat. "You see, I was just a young lad when I got my first job in a small theater in New York City. A stagehand I was. Repaired ropes and hangings and made sure everything was in tip-top shape. To me, it was a magical kingdom. The costumes of every color of the rainbow and the story that came to life. Then there was the smell of greasepaint and the stage settings. Nothing like the theater had ever entered my realm of existence before."

Cici sat mesmerized as he gazed off across the lawn as though he'd entered another world.

"The star of that first show was Ferdie Swaine. He made me believe he was every character he played. Never in my wildest dreams did I think I'd ever be on the stage myself. Then Ferdie's valet came down with a fever, and Ferdie asked me to take his place until he was well again. One of my duties was to read off all the other parts as he practiced his lines." A fit of coughing overcame him for a moment, and Jimmy poured him a glass of water.

"Ah, thank you, my boy." He drank and set the glass down. "Now, where was I?"

"Reading lines, Pops." Blake grinned and his grandfather threw him an affectionate smile.

"But you can stop if you're tired, Da." A burst of laughter followed Mrs. Nelson's remark.

What a loving and fun family they all were.

Jimmy leaned over and whispered in Cici's ear, "You notice she's switched from Papa to Da. She does that every time he tells stories of the old day. I think it takes her back to her childhood."

"That's all right, daughter. I'll go on." He patted Cici's hand again. "Don't want to disappoint this pretty lass."

Cici smiled, in awe of the former vaudeville star. "Thank you, Pops."

"Now, I've lost me train of thought again." He frowned and threw his daughter a scolding look. "Ah yes. I was reading lines for Ferdie, I was. Well, I got to liking it, I did. And Ferdie kept bragging on me to the manager. When it came time for tryouts for the next show, he asked me to read for a small part, so I did. And got the part. Soon they discovered I had a knack for song and dance, and that's when my vaudeville days began."

"Tell her about the Irish troupe, Pops." Blake pursed his lips and Cici had a hunch he was egging on his grandfather to tease his mother.

"Ah yes. She'll be wanting to know about that." Shadows clouded his eyes for a moment. He cleared his throat. "After my wife passed away, I brought my young daughter to her grandparents' farm and came to Chicago looking for work. Vaudeville hadn't reached the area at that time, but the theater district was booming. I was hired by Harrigan's Music Hall and Theater. An Irish troupe they were, with all the old Irish song and dance and musical comedy thrown in. Harrigan himself was a fine Irishman, with a song in his heart and music in his toes. He knew how to put on a show, he did. The Irish weren't too well thought of in this city at that time, but everyone, rich and poor, loved Harrigan and his Irish troupe." His speech slowed and his eyes drooped. "Ah yes, there never was a man like Harrigan...."

A soft snore reached Cici's ear. Why, the old dear. He'd gone to sleep right in the middle of his story.

Dusk was falling as Cici sank back into the seat of Blake's automobile. He'd insisted Jimmy use it to take her home. It had been a full, wonderful day, but the excitement of meeting the extended family had been tiring, and Cici sighed as relaxation engulfed her body.

"Tired?" Jimmy smiled and took her hand.

"Mm-hmm." Then she sat up straight, wide awake. "Shouldn't you have both hands on the steering wheel?"

He bit his lips and grinned but put his hand back on the wheel. "I'm only going about five miles an hour. I don't think we'll crash. But I'm sorry if I made you nervous."

She scooted a little closer to him. "It's all right. I'm not used to automobiles. I'm sure you wouldn't do anything unsafe."

They pulled up to the curb in front of the parsonage and Jimmy came around to Cici's door and helped her out.

As they stood in front of the door, Cici looked up into his eyes. "Thank you for inviting me to the picnic. Your family is very nice."

"They like you, too, Cici. I could tell." He took her hand and smiled. "Is it okay now that I'm not driving?"

She blushed. "Sorry I overreacted."

"I was teasing. You had every right to react to careless driving."

She swayed and he steadied her. "Oh, I must be more tired than I thought. I'd better get inside."

"Thank you for coming with me to the picnic. I'll see you at church in the morning."

"Yes, I'll see you then."

"Don't forget we're going out for lunch."

"I haven't forgotten." She smiled a rather sleepy smile. "Good night, Jimmy." She slipped inside and leaned against the door, listening to his footsteps as he walked across the porch and down the steps.

❧

Jimmy laughed. What a great weekend. He lifted a box and stacked it on some others near the loading area. The picnic had been a great success. Everyone loved Cici and she'd seemed to return the feeling. She'd laughed and talked about Pops all the way home in Blake's new Ford Runabout. He'd almost kissed her good night but decided he'd better not. He didn't want to ruin a perfect day by possibly offending her.

He looked up as the *Lady Fair* bumped against the dock

then watched as the crew lowered the gangplank. The *Lady Fair* was cargo only this trip, so no passengers disembarked. Jimmy and several other stevedores walked on board and began to unload crates.

After church on Sunday, Jimmy and Cici had gone to a restaurant with Eddy and Helen. The girls had been silent most of the evening and rather cool, though polite, to one another. But then after they'd parted company with the other couple, Jimmy and Cici sat on her front porch late into the night, discussing their families and the picnic. Cici told him how much she admired Danielle.

Jimmy had forgotten his concern about Cici and Helen. But now it wormed its way into his thoughts. They'd probably just had a disagreement about something. Jimmy grinned. Girls. Yes, it had been a perfect weekend.

The *Eastland* was coming into the harbor. Good. He hadn't seen Cobb in days. Maybe they could eat their midday meal together. After the *Lady Fair* was unloaded, Jimmy and two others reloaded the ship. Then Jimmy grabbed his lunch bucket from the shack and went looking for Cobb.

A streetcar stopped at the end of the bridge and a tall man stepped off.

Jimmy took in a sharp breath. Sutton. Jimmy's eyes followed him as he hurried down the street in the direction of his old headquarters. Did he still own the place? Jimmy's chest tightened. He turned and almost ran into Cobb, who reached out a hand to steady him.

"Whoa, Jimbo, easy there. What's got you riled up?" Cobb pushed his hat toward the back of his head.

"I just saw Sutton. And there's no mistake. It's him, all right."

"Jimmy, Jimmy. Don't you think I'd have run into him by now if he was in this area?"

"I don't know, Cobb. But it was him," Jimmy snapped. "Why don't we go to the old place now and see if he's there?"

Near panic crossed Cobb's face. "Sorry, Jimbo. We're leaving out again in a few hours. I have to restock the galley. I'll see you when I get back. Maybe we could check it out then." He took off across the dock.

Jimmy's stomach clenched. Cobb was keeping something from him. What if he was mixed up in something illegal with Sutton again?

At least ten children, of all ages, were waiting at the edge of the dock.

Uh-oh. He'd brought a lot of food but didn't know if it would stretch that far. "Hi, gang." He grinned and sat on the old barrel.

A chorus of hellos answered. Bridget and her brothers drew close. At least their lips weren't blue from the cold anymore.

Jimmy managed to find enough for everyone to have a few bites. The children nibbled their food and listened eagerly as Jimmy told the story of David the shepherd boy.

"And he really killed the old mean giant with a little rock?"

"Yes, he really did." Jimmy smiled at the thin, ragged boy who'd asked the question. "But you have to remember, Tom, no one could kill a giant with a stone without help from God. David loved the Lord with all his heart. He knew the Philistines were evil men, out to destroy God's people. He trusted God to help him."

"Why don't God help me, Jimmy?" The little girl was only four. Her mother managed to bring in a little money doing people's laundry, but her husband squandered most of it at a local saloon.

Bridget put her arm around the child's thin shoulders. "But He does help you, Sally. He helps all of us. He sent Jimmy to us, didn't He?"

Jimmy's heart lurched. He had to do more. These children needed more than he could give them from his lunch pail.

God, show me what to do.

Heart heavy, he rode the streetcar home. He'd talk to Rev. Willow. Maybe he'd have some ideas. Or perhaps some of Blake's wealthy friends would be willing to help. He hated to ask, but the children needed so much more than he could give them.

Every time he looked into a hungry face, he remembered that day on the dock after his mother had died and he and Danni had been tossed out onto the street by the woman who had claimed to be her friend. Danni had stolen food that day. She'd done it for him. And Jimmy had never forgotten.

ten

"Sir, I've never experienced this before." Jimmy paced the floor in the parsonage study and searched for the words to convey his thoughts to his spiritual mentor and pastor. He'd struggled all morning with a restlessness he couldn't explain as he helped load the *Midnight Maid*. His thoughts whirled. What was wrong with him? "Maybe I'm not really saved." He flung himself into the chair in front of his pastor's desk.

Rev. Willow steepled his hands and studied Jimmy. "So are you saying you're unsure of your salvation?"

Jimmy sighed and rubbed his finger across the bridge of his nose. "No, no. Not really. I know better. I meant it when I asked Jesus to be my Savior."

The reverend was silent, waiting for Jimmy to gather his thoughts.

"I don't understand why children must suffer. My heart has a longing. A longing to do something meaningful. To show people, especially children, the way out of their misery."

"Rescue the perishing perhaps?" Rev. Willow spoke softly. "That's more than a hymn, you know. It's a direct command from our Lord."

"Yes, maybe that's it. But in more than one sense. It's hard to make children understand that Jesus loves them when their stomachs are hollow from lack of food. Or to help a mother believe when she has no warm blanket for her child."

"It sounds like you have a missionary's heart, Jimmy. Perhaps God has placed this call on your life."

"You mean like going to Africa?" Jimmy's heart fell. He had no desire whatsoever to go to Africa.

"No, no, not necessarily." The reverend smiled. "There's a mission field right in front of you. There in the tenements near the docks. As you say, it's difficult for a starving child, or adult for that matter, to concentrate on spiritual things."

Jimmy sat up straight. A missionary to his people. For they were his people. Always had been. His eyes brimmed with moisture. Soft laughter rolled from his throat. "Rev. Willow, that's it." He smiled at his teacher. "Thank you."

"I did nothing, Jimmy. God led you to this moment. He used me only as a tool."

"What do I do next?" Jimmy laughed. "I have no idea how to be a missionary."

"You are already a missionary. Every time you feed a hungry child or tell one of your Bible stories, you are doing the work of missions. I suggest you continue with your studies. Spend much time in prayer and praise to God. Listen for His voice. Watch for opportunities to serve. Our Lord will let you know when it is time for the next step."

"Seminary?" Jimmy whispered.

Rev. Willow nodded. "I believe so. Unless God tells you otherwise. There is a very good missions program at my old seminary, and it is only a few miles away. If you would like, I'll refer you when the time is right."

"I'd like that very much." Jimmy felt a grin forming. He couldn't wait to tell Cici.

The reverend gazed deep into Jimmy's eyes. "Don't think this is going to be easy, son. You must be very close to God so you can hear His voice. People need help. But their self-esteem must not be crushed."

Jimmy nodded. "How do I prevent that, sir?"

"See them as Jesus sees them. Love them with His unconditional love. Follow His voice and trust Him with the results."

Jimmy jumped up and shook the reverend's hand. "I have to get back to work. Thank you, sir."

He turned away and almost bumped into Cici as he left the room.

Her face was pale and tears filled her eyes.

"Cici, what's wrong?"

"Nothing's wrong. I. . .I must have gotten something in my eyes when I was outdoors."

Without thinking, he grabbed her shoulders. "Cici, you'll never guess. I'm pretty sure I'm supposed to enter seminary and become a missionary."

"A. . .a missionary?"

"Yes, to the poor people of our own city. Isn't it wonderful? God is marvelous!"

A tremulous smile appeared on her face. "Yes, yes, of course. Wonderful, Jimmy."

"I have to get back to work. Do you mind if I come over later so we can talk?"

"Oh. . .I'm sorry, Jimmy. I'm not feeling well. I should probably go to bed."

"Oh, my dear, I'm so sorry. Of course you need to rest and get better." He gripped her hand for a moment then slipped out the front door.

❧

She couldn't believe it. Jimmy had so much going for him. And he wanted to throw it all away to be a preacher? A pang of guilt shot through her. Her father did so much good. There was no doubt he was called to be a minister. But that was different.

Cici got off the streetcar and made her way to Tony's Place. She'd already tried Gail's apartment and several of their friends' homes. This was the last place she could think of where Gail might be. And Cici absolutely had to talk to her.

She pushed through the door, barely missing a waiter in her rush. The tray he held aloft wobbled before he got it balanced. "I'm sorry." Cici gave him an apologetic smile and got a frown in return.

Gail looked up from their usual table and spotted Cici bearing down on them. She said something to the man across from her.

He laughed and left the table just as Cici reached them.

"Well, Cici, sit down and cool off. You look upset."

Cici dropped into the chair the man had vacated and huffed.

"Okay, what's he done this time?"

"Who?"

Gail laughed. "The only one who can get you that stressed out is dear Jimmy. So what's he done?"

Cici waited until the waiter had taken her order for coffee before answering. "I don't know what Jimmy is thinking. I don't understand him at all."

When Gail was silent, Cici sighed. "He's thinking about becoming a missionary."

Laughter exploded from Gail's lips.

"It's not funny, Gail." Cici frowned her displeasure and Gail pressed her hand against her mouth.

"Okay, okay. Sorry." She reached over and patted Cici's hand. "Now, tell me all about it. What else?"

"What else?" Cici straightened and frowned. "Isn't that enough?"

"So do you mean he's going over to Africa to convert natives?"

"No, no. He thinks the docks and all that tenement area is his mission field."

"Oh, well, he already does that. What's the big problem?"

"He's going to seminary. He wants to be a full-time missionary." The despair in Cici's heart rang out in her words.

Gail shook her head in disbelief. "I thought he was supposed to be some kind of lawyer."

"A law school student. A year and a half and he's throwing it away. I thought for sure a few weeks working on the docks would bring him to his senses, but. . ." Cici's words faded and she bit her lip.

"Hmm. I understand why you're so upset. A lawyer's wife has a lot more going for her than a missionary's wife. Don't you think it's time to look around at other options?"

"What? Oh, you mean the fellows in our crowd. I told you before, I'm not interested."

Gail's voice dropped in a conspiratorial manner. "Maybe I meant someone else."

"Who?" Not that she cared, of course. She wasn't interested in anyone but Jimmy. Gail didn't understand. It wasn't so much that Cici wanted to be married to a lawyer. She simply did not want to be married to a preacher. No matter what he called himself. She'd spent all her life so far as a preacher's daughter. Everything was "Don't do this. Be careful what you say. Don't offend anyone. Don't bring shame on your Lord. Don't. Don't. Don't." Maybe her mother liked being a preacher's wife, but Cici wasn't her mother. Pain shot through her. If only she were more like Mama.

"Never mind who." Gail no longer whispered. She smiled. "Hello, Sutton."

Cici looked up.

Sutton stopped beside their table. "Good afternoon, ladies." He bowed over Gail's hand, then took Cici's and lingered over it for a moment. "How very nice to see you, Cecilia."

The pulse in Cici's wrist fluttered, and she cleared her throat. "Hello, Mr. Sutton."

"Tsk-tsk. Now what have I told you? James, not Mr. Sutton." He waved a finger in her direction.

"James." Cici blushed. She had been taught it was disrespectful to address older persons by their given names. Probably another old-fashioned rule she needed to get past. Anyway, Sutton didn't seem all that old.

He seated himself and asked the waiter for a glass of water. "I understand you are interested in the theater, Cecilia."

"Oh, I suppose I am." She had never been to a show in

her life until she'd met Gail, and some of those made her uncomfortable. "An acquaintance of mine used to be in vaudeville. And my friend Jimmy's sister was in a musical comedy a few years ago. Written by her husband."

His eyes flickered and he stared at her. "Oh? And do you by any chance know the title of this musical comedy?"

"Yes, *Peg in Dreamland*. It was the only one he ever wrote professionally."

Anger flared in Sutton's eyes then was gone.

Had she imagined it?

He took a deep breath and seemed to study her. "That is very interesting, my dear. Perhaps you have entertained thoughts of acting as well?"

Now, how had he guessed that? She'd thought of hardly anything else since she'd met Michael O'Shannon and the Nelsons. That is, until Jimmy had told her about his intentions. Why couldn't he have had stars in his eyes about the theater or something like that? Why did he have to be a missionary?

"Cecilia?"

She started, and heat washed over her face. "Oh, I beg your pardon. My thoughts wandered for a moment."

"That's quite all right, my dear." He smiled.

"In answer to your question, I must admit the thought has crossed my mind. But of course it's just nonsense. I could never be an actress."

"Nonsense." His eyes gleamed. "With your beauty and your lovely voice, you could be a star in no time. Perhaps you simply need the right contacts."

"Sutton?" Gail leaned forward, a worried expression in her eyes.

He turned to her, his eyes darkening. "Yes, Gail, dear?"

"N—nothing."

Was that fear in Gail's eyes? But why?

He nodded and a chill went over Cici as he turned his

attention back to her.

Oh, she was only being silly. Why would Gail be afraid of Sutton? They were very close friends.

Sutton called a waiter to refill their glasses. After the waiter had left, Sutton turned to Cici. "While I have focused my directing talents on European cities, I do happen to have several contacts who, I am quite certain, would love to help you find a place in the theater. That is, if you are interested."

Heat washed over Cici. It started at the top of her head and slid downward until even her toes tingled. She stared at him. "Are you serious?"

"Very serious." He took her hand. "Your loveliness would grace any stage, my dear."

"But I've no experience. I've never acted in my life."

He shrugged. "Acting can be taught. You have beauty and presence. That is enough to begin with."

Visions swirled in her thoughts. Her? On the stage? Wearing beautiful dresses? Wined and dined by admirers, flowers thrown at her feet? But what would Mama and Papa say? This wasn't something that could be hidden the way she had hidden her new friends. They would know.

Dread clutched at her stomach, pushing out the excitement that had shot through her a moment before. Mama and Papa would be mortified if word got around, which it surely would. But Danni had been on the stage. And Danni was a wonderful Christian. Mama and Papa were very old-fashioned. Not that there was anything wrong with that. But Sutton cleared his throat and she looked up, startled. "So what is your decision, my dear? Would you like me to look into this for you? It's entirely up to you."

Cici licked her lips. "Could I think about it awhile?"

"Of course." He laughed. "There is no time limit, my dear. My theater contacts will not go away. Take all the time you like."

❧

Jimmy stood by the dock, a large cloth-covered basket on his arm, and peered down the street. He put his hand above his eyes to shield them from the glare of the setting sun that had yet to slip below the horizon.

In the middle of the next block, a group of children huddled around something.

Jimmy couldn't tell what. Laughter reached him and he breathed a sigh of relief.

A head popped up and looked his way, revealing Patrick's grinning face. When he caught sight of Jimmy, he yelled and came running. By the time he reached Jimmy, the others had caught up with him. "Hey, Jimmy. Whatcha doin' down here?"

"Whatcha got in the basket, Jimmy?"

A cacophony of shouts almost drowned each other out.

Jimmy laughed and looked into the basket. "Bread and soup beans. I had extra and wanted to share. Would you mind taking some home with you?"

At the sound of silence, he looked up into blank faces. One of the older boys turned and walked away. Another followed.

"Hey, Walter, where are you going? What's wrong?"

Walter stopped and looked at Jimmy. "My pa'd skin me good if I came home with charity stuff."

"What?" He glanced around. What had he done wrong? "Patrick?"

Patrick licked his lips and looked at the bread. He lifted his eyes to Jimmy's. "Some of the pas don't take nothin' from no one."

Marty Woods, a ten-year-old with a club foot, nodded and shifted on his crutch. "My pa says we may be poor, but we ain't beggars." He hobbled down the street and turned into a narrow alley.

Jimmy glanced around at the children who had remained. "I'm sorry if I've done something wrong. I didn't know."

Lily Rose, a seven-year-old, gave him a sweet smile. "It's okay. Most of us don't have pas." She looked at the basket.

"That bread smells mighty good."

He divided the food between the few remaining children. "Hey, Patrick, where's Mike and Bridget?"

"Bridget had to clean some fish heads someone gave her for soup. She won't let Mike out of her sight since he ran away."

"Well, there should be enough bread here for a couple of days. Does she know how to make beans?" He wasn't taking anything for granted anymore.

"Sure, she makes the bestest beans in the world." He reached a finger through his greasy locks and scratched.

Jimmy forced himself not to grimace as his scalp crawled in response to the sight. Did the boy have lice?

After the Bible story, the children shouted their good-byes and scattered.

Jimmy tromped to the bridge to catch the streetcar. He'd made a mistake today. It didn't matter that he had good intentions. Why had he thought God had called him to feed the hungry and save their souls? It must have been his imagination. How could he help anyone when he had no idea what he was doing?

His heart lurched at the memory of Lily Rose's tiny hand on his. And Patrick and the other children had sat still, their eyes wide as he told them the story of the boy Jesus in the temple.

Hope shot through him. He absolutely was called to help these people. He simply needed someone to guide him.

There used to be a church around here somewhere. Mama used to take him and Danni. They'd know the minds of these people. But where was it? Maybe Danni would remember. Yes. He'd ask Danni.

eleven

"Thank you for inviting me to lunch, Danielle." Cici smiled and sipped her tea.

"It's my pleasure entirely, I assure you." Jimmy's sister put a cube of sugar in her cup and stirred. "I was so disappointed we didn't get a chance to talk alone at the picnic."

"Me, too. But I must admit I enjoyed Mr. O'Shannon's, or rather Pops's, colorful stories of his vaudeville days."

Laughter exploded from Danielle's lips. "I should warn you, the stories often vary in detail. I believe he may have forgotten which versions are the true ones. But he's a wonderful man with a great big heart."

"Yes, I'm sure he is." Cici stirred her tea. Should she broach the subject of Danielle's short acting career? Or would that be rude?

"Is something bothering you?" Danielle pursed her lips, and twin furrows appeared between her eyebrows.

"Oh no. I was just wondering. . .that is, I understand you and your husband were involved with the theater as well."

"That's right. We were for a short while. He wrote a musical comedy and I played the lead." She grinned. "But then we fell in love and he decided he should return to law school and his father's firm."

"He quit law school, too? Like Jimmy?"

"Mm-hmm. He had his heart set on a career in music and the theater. He still loves it but soon came to realize he loved law just as much." She grinned. "His mother was in a show once, too."

"Really? Mrs. Nelson? I mean the senior one?"

"That's the one. She was employed at Harrigan's with her

father until the fire wiped everything out. By that time, she realized all she really wanted to be was Sam Nelson's wife. So she gave it all up."

"He gave her an ultimatum?" Cici felt a spark of anger.

"No—goodness, no. Sam Nelson would have given Kathryn O'Shannon the moon if she'd asked for it. It was all her idea. When the theater was rebuilt, Pops went back though."

"I don't remember ever hearing of Harrigan's. Is it still around?"

"No, I believe there's a nightclub in that spot now. About five years after the fire, Harrigan and his Irish troupe began touring all over the United States and Europe. That's when Pops gave it up. He didn't want to leave his little grandson, Blake." She smiled and winked. "They've always been very close."

Cici took a sighing breath. "I had hoped Jimmy would return to law school."

"Yes, me, too. In fact, I almost begged him. But if he really has a call of God on his life, we wouldn't want to interfere, would we?" Danielle's eyebrows lifted.

Huh. A twinge of guilt shot through Cici. She would interfere in a heartbeat if she thought it would do any good. And she wasn't giving up yet. She took another deep breath and smiled. "I suppose not. But tell me, how could you stand to lay it all down? I mean, your career?"

"Oh dear. I have everything I want. Blake is the most important thing in my life, and now"—she smiled and leaned forward, close to Cici—"I'm going to have a baby in October."

"Oh, how exciting. Does Jimmy know?"

"Yes, and he's going to be a wonderful uncle. I know it."

The clock on the mantel chimed twice. Cici smiled and stood. "I really must get back to the parsonage. I promised to help Mother mend choir robes this afternoon."

"Oh dear, and I never got around to asking you."

"Asking me what?" Cici's heart pounded. Had Danielle found out about Gail? But how?

"My church ladies' benevolence group has agreed to sponsor Jimmy's charitable activities in the tenement district." She stood and faced Cici. "We're going to open a soup kitchen down near the Clark Street docks in the near future. When we get more information about the families, we'll be distributing food baskets. I thought perhaps you might like to be involved."

Cici relaxed and smiled. She wasn't really that excited about the idea, but she would have agreed to anything just now. "Yes, I'd like that very much."

"Good, then that's settled. Our first meeting is next Tuesday. I'll pick you up in the carriage." She gave Cici a wide grin. "Blake won't let me touch his Ford, and personally I think it's way too loud anyway."

On the way home, Cici stared out the streetcar window and frowned. How did she let herself get talked into working with the poor? But there was one thing in its favor. Perhaps if she got to know more about the people Jimmy was so concerned about, she'd get some ideas of how to change his mind. After all, she was only thinking about his future. He'd thank her someday. She leaned against the seat and smiled. Yes, this was a good thing.

❧

The little church stood, small and obscure, between two tall buildings, its stones black from grime. Danni said she came here a few years ago. The pastor was new, but he was kind. Perhaps, living in this area, he would understand the people.

Jimmy gave a short laugh. He'd spent the first twelve years of his life here. But after they'd gone to live with Sutton, everything had changed. They were kept pretty close and weren't allowed out much except for the games, sometimes. And then they were in groups. Most of the time, the games were inside. A queasiness came over Jimmy. Games, Sutton called them. Lessons in stealing, that's what they were.

Jimmy knocked on the door. The sun bored into his shoulder blades.

"Come on in. Door's open." The shout echoed from somewhere inside.

Jimmy turned the doorknob and pushed open the door. The smell of paint assaulted his nostrils. The room was dark, shaded by the tall buildings on each side. Benches stood in rows. Pretty rickety. Most of them looked like they were on their last legs. Jimmy scanned them, frowning. Why hadn't anyone fixed them?

"Be right there." The words issued from a narrow door standing open at the rear of the room.

A moment later, a man stepped through. His overalls were spattered with white paint. He came forward, his hand outstretched. "Hello, I'm Brother Paul Norell. How may I help you?"

Jimmy shook the man's hand. "Jimmy Grayson. I work on the docks."

"Grayson." A thoughtful expression crossed his face. "Sounds familiar. Have we met?"

"No, sir. I believe you met my sister, Danielle, a few years ago."

His face lit up. "Of course. Danielle Grayson. And you are her younger brother. She mentioned you."

"Yes. I hope I haven't come at an inconvenient time. I hurried over here when we broke for lunch."

"Not at all. I was about to take a break from painting the kitchen anyway. You've given me the excuse I needed. Here, let's sit." He led the way to a bench up near the pulpit. When they were seated, Brother Paul smiled. "We're not likely to be disturbed. My wife is out replenishing our larder, and seldom does anyone come during the noon hour."

"Er. . .Brother Paul. . ." Jimmy hesitated at the unfamiliar terminology.

"Jimmy, please feel free to call me Paul. We don't stand on formality."

"Paul, then." Jimmy grinned then paused. "I believe I'm called to do missionary work among the people of this area."

Interest sparked in Paul's eyes and he nodded. "Go on."

As Jimmy shared the things on his mind and heart, lightness seemed to lift him from the helplessness he'd walked in the past few days. When he'd finished, relief washed over him and he glanced at Paul.

Paul blew a puff of air from between pursed lips. "Jimmy, you've learned one of the first lessons necessary for ministering to poverty-stricken people. I don't speak of the bums who think the world owes them a living, but people who want with all their hearts to take care of themselves. The only thing they have is their faith in God and their self-respect. As long as they can set a meal on the table for their families, they can keep both. And we mustn't ever intrude on that no matter how much we want to help. Because once they lose their self-respect, their faith soon follows, and after that there's nothing for them to do but give up in despair. Do what you can to protect their self-respect."

"Then what can I do to help them?"

"Pray for them. Feed the children whenever possible. Help those widows and abandoned mothers. Be ready to give an encouraging word to the men, and if an opportunity to help without breaking them should arise, follow the Lord's leading. Assist them to find jobs whenever possible. Most of them will work extra when the chance comes. Do what you can to stop the unfair wages and working conditions. Let God love and help them through you." He paused and took a deep breath. "It isn't easy, Jimmy. Your heart will be broken over and over again. And your patience will be tested time and time again. Be very sure, my friend. And remember, God loves these precious people more than you do. I'll be here to encourage you, pray for you, and help you in any way I can."

"Thank you, Paul. I do have one other question. My sister's church is thinking about opening a soup kitchen and distributing food baskets. Do you think that's a bad idea?"

"On the contrary. It's a very good idea. You will be there for those who want and need help. But you won't be intruding on those who don't. Even the proudest of men will not likely object to their families having bowls of soup for their midday meals as long as they aren't brought into the homes and put before their faces." An eager smile appeared on his face. "I'd like very much to help with this project in any way I can."

Jimmy went back to work with a clearer idea of what was before him and a sense of direction. He'd make mistakes. No doubt of that. But he could see the path now, and having Paul's prayers in addition to Rev. Willow's gave him a sense of peace he hadn't had before.

And faith. Paul's comments about the men and their faith in God had impressed him. If these poor men could have faith in God in their situations, he could certainly learn to trust the Lord in his. And Paul had said the same thing Rev. Willow had. God loved these people more than he did. He would be there to lead and guide in this endeavor.

Two small girls waved from a dingy hallway where they were weaving colored strips of fabric through each other's hair.

"Hi, Jimmy. Where you going?"

Now, what was her name? Oh yes. "Back to work, Brenda. You sure look pretty today. And you look pretty, too, Janey Lee."

Both girls giggled. "Thanks for the cheese and apples you gave us." The little brunette grinned, and the other, with stringy blond hair, nodded and smiled.

"You're very welcome, Janey Lee. You too, Brenda. See you later."

"See you later, Jimmy," Janey Lee shrilled.

"See you later, Jimmy," Brenda echoed.

Why did Danni keep looking at him like that? She'd been throwing him furtive glances all during dinner.

"Is something wrong, Danni?"

She bit her lip and pink slid over her face. She gave a little shake of her head and focused on the enormous slice of chocolate cake that had already shrunk to half its size.

Jimmy shrugged. His imagination more than likely. He resumed his narrative of his midday conversation with Paul Norell.

"That's interesting, Jimmy." Blake, always the encourager, had been on Jimmy's side from the beginning in spite of his disappointment that his brother-in-law wouldn't be practicing law with him. "My father told me a story once about his experiences with the Chicago poor before the great fire, especially immigrants. Many people, including Dad, were under the false impression that they were shiftless people. He discovered most of them weren't. Rather, they were hardworking people forced to live and work under abominable conditions. Things aren't as bad now as back then, but it's still very hard for poor people to earn a living there."

"Yes, there will always be those who take advantage of the less fortunate." Jimmy lifted a bite of his cake to his mouth. A picture of Patrick, Mike, and Bridget came to his mind and he put the fork down.

"Jimmy"—Danni's eyes swam with tears as she stared at his plate—"it won't help any child for you to do without food."

He took a deep breath. "I know. I have to learn to deal with my thoughts though."

"Let's have our coffee in the parlor and talk awhile. We haven't seen much of you lately."

Blake laughed. "Now, Danielle, don't be a mother hen. Remember when we were courting?"

"Humph. I remember when you drilled me for hours on my diction and the position of my head."

"Huh?" Jimmy stared at his sister.

"Don't mind her." Blake snickered and gave a little yank to one of Danni's curls. "She's still holding an eight-year grudge over my coaching techniques for *Peg in Dreamland*."

"I am not."

Danni and Blake stepped into the parlor, laughing while Jimmy trailed behind, shaking his head. It was great the way those two still laughed and teased each other. Would he and Cici be like that when they'd been married that long? He froze. Where did that thought come from? He and Cici hadn't spoken of marriage. But in his heart, he dreamed.

"Come on, Jimmy. Why are you standing in the doorway?"

He laughed and stepped into the room. "A lot on my mind, I guess." He sat in a corner chair by the open window. He leaned back and yawned, closing his eyes for a moment.

"Jimmy."

He jerked up. "Sorry, I must have drifted off to dreamland. Didn't see Peg there."

Blake snorted. "Good one."

Danni wasn't laughing.

"C'mon, Danni. You've been giving me strange looks all evening. What's wrong?"

"I'm not sure if anything is." She bit her lip. "Are you serious about Cici?"

"Danni, that's Jimmy's business." Blake held up both hands at her glare. "Okay."

Jimmy swallowed. "Well, yes, I guess I am. Yes, I am serious. I want to marry her. Haven't proposed yet though. I'm sure she'd think it was much too soon. Besides, I can't really support a wife on a dockworker's salary."

She frowned. "But you'll more than likely have support from a church after seminary, won't you?"

"Yes, hopefully." Jimmy knew he was going to get depressed if this conversation continued.

She bit her lip. "That's not what I wanted to talk about.

What I was wondering is, have you talked to Cici about your ministry?"

"Some. Why?" Now what was she getting at?

"Are you sure Cici shares your enthusiasm for helping the poor?"

Jimmy's heart seemed to drop into his stomach. Was he sure? She'd smiled and said, "That's wonderful," when he'd told her his decision. But her eyes had seemed to say something different.

What if she didn't share his desire to minister to hurting people? He took a deep breath. "I suppose it's time to find out, before it's too late." But was it already too late? Was he willing to give her up for this call on his life?

twelve

Jimmy and Cobb stared after the family struggling down the street. The man's brow was still furrowed with anger as he pushed a wheelbarrow piled high with boxes and bags. Pots and pans stuck out, in danger of falling to the street. The man's exhausted-looking wife carried several crammed-full pillowcases, and the three boys each had a corner of a bulging tied-up sheet that threatened to spill its contents. Other pedestrians avoided the family's eyes as they hurried past, probably thankful it wasn't them.

Jimmy followed, determined to try one more time. "Hawkins, if you won't allow me to give you the money, at least accept a loan."

"Get away from me." He dropped the handles of the wheelbarrow and turned a face filled with fury upon Jimmy. "I don't need your help. It's my family, and I'll take care of them. A man has to take care of his own."

Jimmy stepped back. What could he do? As soon as he'd heard the Hawkinses were being evicted, he'd gone to their home and offered his assistance with the rent. An offer that was promptly refused with a counteroffer to kick Jimmy out the door.

Cobb clapped his hand on Jimmy's shoulder. "Let them go, Jimbo. There ain't nothing you can do."

"But where will they go?" Confusion clouded his mind and grief cut into his heart. Where could they possibly go?

Cobb inhaled a breath and blew it out with a loud *whoosh*. "Don't worry yourself sick over it. They'll find some place."

"How will they do that? They have no money. God, show

me what to do." The words came out with a groan. A groan that seemed to come from the depths of his being. "Those little boys, Lord."

"Okay, Jimbo"—Cobb faced him and grabbed his shoulders—"listen to me. There ain't nothin' you can do. Nothin' at all. Don't take it so hard. You can't help everyone."

The harshness of Cobb's voice penetrated Jimmy's mind. Realization hit like a sledgehammer against a concrete wall. There was nothing he could do. "I'm going home." Home where no one was cold or hungry or homeless.

"Now you're talking. Get some hot food in your stomach and a good night's rest. You'll feel better in the morning. Just wait and see if you don't."

Jimmy sighed. "Yeah, you should be a preacher, Cobb."

"Who, me?" A horrified, trapped expression crossed his face. "Why would I want to do that?"

"Don't look so scared. I was only teasing." He narrowed his eyes and peered at Cobb. "Wouldn't hurt you to go to church though."

"Yeah, that's what you keep telling me." Cobb grinned. "Maybe I will, one of these days. Who knows?"

Jimmy waved and headed for the streetcar line. He rode in silence, hardly noticing the other passengers. Had he only imagined the call of God on his life? He'd stood helpless and watched a family trudge down the street with nowhere to go. Maybe if he'd handled it differently. . ."

He groaned. He'd broken the first rule. Never intrude. Always protect a man's self-respect.

❧

Jimmy moved his fork around his plate, his mind wandering over the events of the afternoon. Emptiness swelled like a cavern inside him. It was over.

"Jimmy, what's wrong? You haven't touched your food." Danni frowned.

"Sorry, sis." He stabbed a piece of pot roast and lifted it to his mouth. The tender, succulent bite may as well have been burnt coal.

"Are you ill?" She pushed her chair back and rose.

"No, I'm fine." He motioned her to return to her seat. "I have some things on my mind. Nothing for you to worry about."

She cast him a glance that said she didn't believe a word of it then continued her conversation with Blake.

After dinner, Jimmy took his brother-in-law aside. "Could I speak with you privately?"

"Of course. Let's go to the study."

Jimmy followed him and they sat in leather chairs on each side of the empty fireplace.

"So it would appear Danielle was right. Something is wrong." Blake raised his eyebrows.

Jimmy drummed his fingers on the round table beside his chair. "I don't know, Blake. I'm having second thoughts about becoming a missionary."

"Are you? Hmm. I thought you were set on the decision." Blake peered at him. "What has brought on this new doubt?"

Jimmy cracked his knuckles, something he hadn't done in years. He took a deep breath. "Several things. I'm not sure I'm cut out for it. Maybe I imagined I heard from God. Besides, I'm seriously thinking of proposing marriage to Cici. How can I ask her to marry a dockworker who can't support her?"

"Okay, Jimmy." Blake leaned forward, his hands planted on his knees. "Something has brought this on. Do you want to tell me about it?"

Jimmy opened his mouth and the incident with the Hawkins family poured out. "All I could do was stand and watch as a whole family carried their belongings down the street, knowing they had nowhere to go."

"So this is about your feeling of helplessness?"

"Partly. But watching that proud man, knowing what his pain must be, I envisioned Cici. Because the same thing could happen to us."

"Jimmy, that's nonsense. You have a home with Danielle and me as long as you need or want it. Cici, too. In fact, Danielle and I sort of discussed it when we heard you wanted to be a missionary to the poor. We have plenty of room."

"I know you mean well, Blake." Jimmy attempted a smile that didn't materialize. "But a man has to take care of his own." He drew in a sharp breath. That was what Hawkins said. He jumped up. That settled it. He knew what he had to do. "I think it would be best for me to return to law school. I'm going to talk to Cici."

The streetcar ride to the parsonage seemed to take forever. Should he propose? But they hadn't really spoken of a future together. Perhaps she was only interested in a companion for recreational purposes. Still, she had agreed to meet his family and close friends and they all got on well. In any case, he'd need to get a ring before he proposed and nothing would be open this late. So that settled it. No proposal tonight.

Knots formed in his stomach as he knocked on the parsonage door. It was after eight. Perhaps the Willows would consider it too late for him to be calling.

"Jimmy, what a pleasant surprise. Come in." Mrs. Willow beamed as she opened the door.

"I hope it isn't too late for me to be calling. I'm afraid I wasn't thinking." Jimmy gave her an apologetic smile as he stepped into the hallway.

"Not at all. Are you here to see my husband or my daughter?" Humor shone from her blue eyes. Eyes so much like Cici's.

"Well, Cici. Of course, she may not be home. I shouldn't have assumed."

"I'm here. Hello, Jimmy." Cici's trilling voice matched the smile on her face. "Would you like to come into the parlor?"

"Uh, yes, I suppose so." If he didn't quit stammering, she'd think he was an idiot.

"Perhaps you young folks would prefer to sit on the porch

swing. It's a lovely night." Mrs. Willow smiled again. "I really must return to my mending."

"The swing is a very good idea, Mama." Cici grinned and practically shoved Jimmy through the door.

He followed her to the swing, where they sat down together, their shoulders nearly touching, which didn't help Jimmy's nerves any.

"I'm so glad you came over, Jimmy. I was beginning to think you'd forgotten me." Her pink lips formed a pout that set Jimmy's heart thumping triple time. "I haven't seen you since Sunday."

Jimmy couldn't suppress a grin. "Today is only Tuesday, you know. Although I must admit it seems much longer to me. But to be honest, I didn't want to wear out my welcome."

Cici dimpled. "Does that mean you wanted to come over yesterday?"

"Of course. I'd be hanging on your doorstep like a lonesome dog if I thought I wouldn't get kicked off."

A peal of laughter erupted from her throat. "All right. I believe you."

"Good." He grinned then relaxed his face. "There is something I'd like to talk to you about."

"Oh?" She lowered her eyes, her lashes brushing her cheeks, but not before he'd seen a flicker of something that appeared to be dread. What was she expecting him to say?

"I'm seriously thinking of returning to law school to complete my studies. I only have six months to go. After that I can work at the Nelson firm while I'm studying for the bar."

Her eyes widened and her lips fell open. "Really? So you've decided not to be a missionary?"

"Almost. I'm still thinking things over."

"But why?" And why was she questioning his decision? Wasn't this what she'd wanted all along?

"I saw a poor family evicted from their home today. I might have helped them if I hadn't handled it wrong." He inhaled a deep breath.

Pain clutched him as he told her about the Hawkins family and about the man's reaction.

"Well, that just goes to show you can't help some people." Indignation filled her voice and a frown creased her forehead. "I know there are deserving people who can't help being poor, but that man was horrible to you."

"But. . .Cici. . ."

"Never mind." She reached over and touched his cheek. "The church ladies will be opening the soup kitchen and you can still give food to the children. That's probably all God ever intended you to do."

He lifted his hand and covered hers. A tingling sensation ran all the way up his arm. It was so precious of her to care about his feelings.

"Cici, I'd like to spend more time with you."

"You would?" A flash of excitement filled her eyes. Why hadn't he bought a ring before now? Perhaps she would have accepted his proposal.

"Yes." He took a deep breath. "I care deeply for you."

A pretty pink blush stained her cheeks.

"Is there any possibility you could return my feelings?"

"I care for you, too." Her whispered words sent joy ringing through him, and he grabbed both her hands and brought them to his lips.

She giggled. "I was beginning to wonder if you'd ever kiss my hand again."

He smiled and lifted her chin. "Not only your hand."

Her lips trembled and he caught his breath. "Cici." He lowered his lips and brushed hers in a soft kiss.

⁊⁊

Cici wrapped her arms around herself as she stared out her window into the moonlight.

Thank You, God. You never meant Jimmy to be a missionary, did You?

Of course He didn't. And now that Jimmy was back on the right track, Cici would be sure to serve God. Yes, she would. The first thing she would do tomorrow would be to call Gail and bow out of her planned afternoon on the *Eastland* with Gail and Sutton. After all, she was quite certain Jimmy would propose soon, and an attorney's wife had to watch her reputation. She hugged herself then whirled around the room, her arms flung wide.

❧

Jimmy stepped off the streetcar, still nearly floating from the time he spent with Cici. He gave a little skip as he headed down the sidewalk. She loved him. He knew she did. If he'd had a ring, he would have proposed and she would have accepted. He was sure of it.

In the morning, he would send word that he'd be late to work and would make the necessary arrangements for returning to school next term. He laughed. Danni would be thrilled. The missionary idea had been a foolish dream.

The faces of Patrick, Mike, and Bridget popped into his mind and he slowed. But of course, he would still do what he could for the children. He would never desert them. And as Cici said, the women's group would have the soup kitchen and the food basket program. But. . .who would sit and tell Bible stories to the children? Who would offer hope for the future?

An agony Jimmy had never known knifed through his heart. Could he walk away? After all this time? He stopped.

"God! What do You want from me?" He hadn't meant to speak out loud, didn't realize he had shouted until an upper shade flew up in the house he faced.

A man leaned out the window. "Quiet down! People are trying to sleep!"

Jimmy lifted his hand in silent apology and resumed his walk home.

The light was still on in the parlor. Jimmy went inside and found Danielle sitting in her rocker with her Bible in her hand. She looked up, a troubled look on her face.

Jimmy flopped down on the sofa across from her.

"Jimmy?"

"Danni, what's wrong with me? I keep making decisions and then having second thoughts." He put his head in his hands.

"Blake told me you were thinking of returning to law school?" She peered at him.

"Yes, I even told Cici."

"And what did she think about the idea?"

"Oh, she was happy. Agreed it would be best. She had a lot of sensible things to say." He took a deep breath. "I could still help the children."

"Uh-huh." She laid the Bible on the side table.

"And your ladies' group is going to help with food and clothing."

"Yes."

"I thought you'd be jumping up and down with joy." He could hear the exasperation in his voice. "Sorry, sis. Didn't mean to snap."

"It's all right, Jimmy. I know you're under a lot of stress right now. Indecision will do that to you."

"I don't know what to do." He groaned, angry with himself for his inability to stick to his plan.

"Jimmy, what do you think is causing this struggle?" She gazed into his eyes.

He lowered his eyes. "Like I told Blake, I feel inadequate for missionary work."

"But you haven't even begun, really. Just because one man rejected your help, you're giving up the dream God placed in your heart?"

"I thought you wanted me to go back to law school." What was wrong with everyone anyway?

"I do. But only if it's God's plan and you want it with your whole heart." She paused. "I've never seen you so happy as you've been lately, Jimmy."

He jumped up. "Thanks for listening, Danni. I'm going up to bed." He kissed her on the cheek and went to his bedroom.

She was right. He had been happy. Why had he let this one incident change his mind? He dropped into a chair by the window and looked out at the moon. The same moon that had looked down as he kissed Cici's soft lips. And the truth hit him.

Will she love me if I don't return to law school? Will she agree to be the wife of a missionary?

thirteen

Rain fell in sheets, slapping the parlor window where Jimmy stood. A flash of lightning speared the ground, followed by a clap of thunder that shook the room.

"Great, just great." What else could happen? Just before his shift ended, a badly tied-up barrel had fallen from the mast of the *Eastern Sun*, bursting its contents, which happened to be molasses, all over the deck. And naturally he had to help with the cleanup. The jeweler had been locking up when Jimmy arrived and it had taken ten minutes to talk the man into letting him purchase a ring. Only when Jimmy had pulled out his money did the store owner relent and let him in.

Jimmy drew in a deep breath and let it out with a huff. He pulled the little blue box from his vest pocket and looked at it again. Would Cici like it? Was the stone big enough? He'd had a little money saved up. But when he'd glanced over the rings and seen the prices, he'd almost walked out. He'd finally chosen one he thought she'd like that hadn't been too much more than he'd planned to spend. Now that he examined it more closely, he wasn't sure. It was the new Edwardian style with a platinum band. He sighed and put it back in his pocket. He never would find out, if the rain didn't stop. He'd thought of making a run for it, but he'd be soaked before he got to the streetcar line. Maybe he'd better call Cici and tell her he couldn't make it.

"Jimmy, why are you standing in the dark?" Blake turned on the gas lamp on the wall by the door. "I thought you'd already left."

Jimmy shook his head. "In this downpour? I'd be half drowned before I got half a block."

"You can take the carriage. I've told you before to feel free to use it anytime Danielle doesn't need it."

"Maybe I'll wait until it slacks up and take the umbrella." Jimmy preferred the more modern style of transportation. It freed him from making arrangements for the horse. And Blake sure hadn't offered his automobile. Probably afraid Jimmy would wreck it on the slippery streets.

"Okay, I offered." Blake sighed and shook his head. "Oh, all right. Take the Runabout."

Jimmy grinned and looked out the window. "Nah, it's letting up. I think I'll make a run for the streetcar. See you later."

He grabbed his umbrella from the stand in the foyer and took off down the street. He'd only been waiting a couple of minutes when the streetcar arrived. Maybe his luck was turning. Or. . .maybe God had something to do with it. Uneasiness churned in his stomach as he climbed aboard the public conveyance. He hadn't been spending much time with God. It wasn't that he was turning away from Him or anything like that. He'd just been busy. Too busy to spend an hour or even a few minutes with God? He hadn't had his Bible open all week except at church. He pushed the thought aside and took a seat in the empty car. Apparently he was the only one crazy enough to come out in this weather.

By the time he got off near the parsonage, the rain had increased again, so Jimmy opened his umbrella and ran down the sidewalk in the deluge.

Cici's eyes widened as she opened the door for him. "Jimmy, I didn't think you'd come."

"I told you I'd be here." He grinned, shook the umbrella, and propped it up by the door, then wiped his feet on the mat.

"Well, get in here. You look like a drowned cat." She giggled and pulled him inside, shutting the door behind him.

"I don't know, Cici. Maybe I should stay on the porch. Your mother might not be too happy with my dripping all over the place." He grinned. "Besides, I need to speak to you privately."

"Oh, all right." She smiled then called out, "Mother, I'm sitting on the porch with Jimmy."

Mrs. Willow stepped from the parlor. "Oh my. Perhaps Jimmy should come in the kitchen and get dried off."

"I'm fine, ma'am. I'll just get soaked again in a few minutes when I leave."

"Well, my goodness, young man. Why did you come out in this weather if you're only staying a few minutes?"

"Mama. . ." Cici threw her mother a pleading look.

"I'd best return to my knitting. I'm making socks for the children in the tenements."

"That's nice, Mrs. Willow. I'm sure they'll be appreciated."

When they were finally seated on the porch swing, Jimmy leaned back and took her hand. She smiled up at him.

"Cici, honey, you must know that I love you." He laid his hand on her cheek. "And I pray you have feelings for me as well."

A pink blush kissed her cheeks. She ducked her head then looked straight up at him. "I love you, too, Jimmy."

Joy filled his heart and he slipped out of the swing and onto one knee. He ran his tongue over his suddenly dry lips and took a deep breath. "Will you marry me?"

Cici gasped. With her eyes wide and bright with tears, she flung her arms around his neck. "Oh yes, Jimmy. I want to be your wife more than anything in the world."

His hands trembled as he put the ring on her finger. Then he sat beside her and took her into his arms.

"It's beautiful. The most beautiful ring I've ever seen." Cici held her hand out and admired the ring. "Jimmy, it's a diamond."

He grinned. "Diamonds are all the style for engagement rings now. Are you sure you like it? I can exchange it for one with a different stone if you'd rather."

She covered the ring with her other hand as if to protect it.

"I'll never part with this ring as long as I live." Her upturned lips were too much to resist.

"You are precious." Jimmy kissed softly at first, then deepened the kiss until she drew back, trembling.

Jimmy barely noticed his damp clothing as the hours passed and they declared their love for each other over and over again. It was nearly midnight when he arrived home. He climbed the stairs, reliving the evening, examining every word, every kiss. Yes, he'd done the right thing. He had the most precious fiancée who ever lived and no one had ever loved the way they did.

But as he got ready for bed, the thought he'd kept at bay finally forced its way into his mind. What would she say if she knew he hadn't yet made arrangements to return to school?

&

Silver tinkled against twinkling crystal. Soft candlelight bathed the white tablecloth and red napkins with a romantic ambience, perfect for this night.

Cici blushed and bit her lip as Jimmy sent her an adoring smile across the table. "Jimmy, don't look at me like that. People will notice." Her whispered words didn't reflect the delight that coursed through her being.

"Well, I guess I don't care if you don't." He grinned and reached across the table, taking her hand. He ran his thumb across the diamond, which appeared enormous to Cici as it winked in the candlelight.

"Behave yourself." She slipped her hand from his and darted a glance around the room.

"There, you see? No one is paying the least bit of attention."

He was right. They could have been on an island for all the attention they were getting. Even the waiter seemed to know they wanted solitude and only appeared when it was time for another course of the excellent meal or to refill their water glasses.

When the last delicious bite was eaten, they lingered over their tea until finally Jimmy rose. "We'd better be getting to the theater. We don't want to miss the opening act."

Cici's heart thumped hard against her rib cage. When she'd suggested to Jimmy that they go to see the new musical comedy, it had seemed like a great adventure. After all, she'd never been to the theater. But as they walked into the luxurious, sparkling lobby, she swallowed past a lump and darted a glance around. What if some of her parents' friends should see her? Of course they wouldn't have any right to talk if they were here. But what if someone mentioned seeing her here to her parents, just in passing? Her father and mother never judged others for theatergoing, but her father often said a minister and his family must be above reproach.

"Honey, what are you so nervous about?" Jimmy squeezed her elbow and she drew closer to him and smiled.

"I'm not nervous. Just looking around. This is my first time at a play."

"Really? If I'd known that, we could have come sooner."

How was she going to get it across to him not to mention this to her parents? What would he think of her when he found out she was going against her father's wishes? But she was an adult. Soon to be an attorney's wife. She needed to learn how to conduct herself in society.

"Perhaps we should have invited your parents to join us."

Cici drew her breath in sharply then calmed herself. "Yes, that would have been very nice. Perhaps another time." She sank into the luxurious seat. How could anything be so superbly comfortable? Red velvet curtains hung from some secret place near the vast ceiling. Golden cords hung down on each side. Surely this must be dreamland.

The theater filled up to capacity and the lights went off.

Cici sat mesmerized as the curtains rose on a bright, colorful kingdom where not only birds sang their songs to one another, but people did, too.

During intermission, Jimmy excused himself for a moment, but Cici sat glued to her chair, afraid of missing even one magical moment.

A young woman in a frilly blue dress stepped out on the stage and sang a song while waiting for the crowd to return.

When Jimmy returned to his seat, Cici clutched his arm and smiled.

"Enjoying your first show, sweetheart?" He squeezed her hand.

"Oh yes. It's wonderful and amazing. I can't imagine why. . ." She stopped herself before giving her secret away. But why did her parents think the theater was inappropriate?

When the curtain came down after the final act, Cici applauded with everyone else and then followed Jimmy down the aisle, almost in a daze. She blinked in the bright electric lights of the chandelier in the lobby.

Jimmy guided her through the crowd toward the door then suddenly stopped, almost jerking Cici to a halt.

She gasped as she saw Sutton facing them.

He swept an amused glance in her direction then turned his attention to Jimmy. "Well, Jimmy, my boy, it's been a long time." He pressed his lips together and nodded. "Much too long. It's always good to see one of my children."

Cici gazed at Jimmy in wonder. A muscle by his mouth jumped as he stared at Sutton in stony silence.

"Tell me, Jimmy"—Sutton's eyes burned and Cici could see fury in their depths—"how is the lovely Danielle? Please give her my love and tell her I'll be seeing you both very soon."

Jimmy clutched Cici's arm and pushed past him. His breath came in ragged bursts, his face tense with anger. Silently, he hailed a carriage and held the door for Cici.

She climbed in, not speaking until he was seated beside her. "Jimmy, what's wrong? Did you know that man?" Of course Jimmy knew him. Sutton had called him and Danielle by name.

Jimmy inhaled deeply and turned to her. He smiled. "Don't worry about him. He's a very unpleasant person whom I hope you never have to see again."

Unpleasant? She wouldn't call Sutton unpleasant. He'd always been very gracious to her. But of course, Jimmy mustn't know she was acquainted with a man he was obviously at enmity with. She waited, hoping he would reveal how he knew Sutton. Why had the man called Jimmy one of his children?

"I hope you enjoyed the evening, sweetheart. I'm sorry if the last incident hindered your enjoyment in any way."

"No, no. Not at all." She hesitated, not sure how to broach the subject of her parents. "Jimmy, I wonder if you would mind not mentioning that we went to the theater. To Mama and Papa, I mean."

Astonishment crossed his face. "What? Why ever not?"

Heat filled her face. "It's just that, you see, they wouldn't approve of my going."

A sick look crossed his face.

Cici felt tears surfacing. Oh no. He would hate her now.

"Cici—" His voice broke. "Why didn't you tell me? Or for that matter, why." He stopped, but disappointment clouded his eyes.

"I'm sorry, Jimmy. But I wanted to see a show so badly. I know it was wrong to go against my parents' wishes."

He slipped his arm around her and kissed the top of her head. "Well, what's done is done. I love you, sweetheart."

"I love you, too." The words came out in a sob. "I love you so much."

≈

Jimmy sent the carriage away and took the streetcar home. The clacking sound of the wooden seats and *rickety-racketing* of the wheels grated on his nerves. The jerking of the car, which he usually didn't notice, caused his head to pound.

He had frozen at the sight of Sutton. And when the evil

rascal dared to mention Danielle's name, all Jimmy wanted to do was put his hands around the evil man's neck and squeeze the life out of him. Had he ever been angry enough to willingly consider violence? He didn't think so.

It was obvious Sutton had a plan that involved Jimmy and his sister. Jimmy knew the man well enough to know the plan wasn't a benevolent one. He was set on revenge, and there was no telling what measure he would take to achieve his goal. Jimmy also hadn't liked the way the man's eyes had wandered over Cici.

And that was another thing. Why would Cici have asked Jimmy to take her to the theater when she knew her parents would not approve? What did that say about her character? Guilt bit at him at the thought. There was nothing wrong with Cici's character. She was still very young. It was simply a girlish whim.

When he entered the house, his eyes wandered up the stairs. Should he wake Blake? Warn him about Sutton? But what good would it do to rob him of a night's sleep? There was nothing Danni's and his former captor could do here in their own home. He'd make sure he spoke to Blake in the morning and leave it up to him what to say to Danni.

He practically dragged himself up the stairs. He changed into his pajamas and robe then threw himself into a chair.

God, I don't know what to do.

But his words seemed to fall like stones on the carpeted floor, muffled and going nowhere. How could he come to God when his conscience was stabbing him so? When the eyes of the tenement children haunted him? Their voices called to him when he slept.

He groaned and stepped to the window. Moonlight streamed in, enveloping the room in a ghostly aura. He jerked the curtains shut and climbed into bed. This should have been a day of delirious happiness for him and Cici. Instead, his whole world seemed to be caving in.

fourteen

"Jimmy, when you complete your studies, you'll need to begin studying for the bar right away. You'll find everything you need here in my library and the one at the office." Mr. Nelson sank into a leather armchair and motioned for Blake and Jimmy to do likewise.

"Thank you, sir." His stomach sank, as it always did lately, at the mention of his career in law.

"What's on your mind, son?" Mr. Nelson had an observant eye and little got by him.

Jimmy opened his mouth to deny anything was wrong, but the words wouldn't come. He sighed. "I can't stop thinking of the conditions in the slums by the river, especially around the Clark Street docks. I feel that I've deserted those people."

Blake leaned forward. "But you're still feeding the children from your own lunch pail every day as well as taking food to pass out on Saturdays."

"I know, but it doesn't seem near enough."

"Are you reconsidering your decision to return to law school? I notice you've not made the arrangements yet." Mr. Nelson stretched his feet and legs onto the leather ottoman.

"Jimmy?" Blake raised his eyebrows in question.

"I'm not sure. But I can't get the poor tenement people off my mind."

They spent an hour discussing the law firm and various pending cases, then talked about a recent fishing trip on which Blake and his father caught several large bass.

Finally, Mr. Nelson rose. "Katie will kill me if I keep you to myself any longer. We'd best join the women in the parlor. Tea sounds good anyway."

Blake and Jimmy followed the older man from the room.

"Oh good. You're here." Mrs. Nelson crinkled her eyes and smiled at her husband, who bent and kissed her brow.

Jimmy glanced at Cici, who smiled and patted the cushion next to her on the sofa.

"Jimmy, I'm so glad you came today and brought Cecilia." Mrs. Nelson smiled and turned to Cici. "He used to join us for Sunday dinner every week. But now"—she sent a teasing smile Cici's way—"he seems to have other things to do."

Jimmy grinned. "I'm sure we'll be here more often now that we're engaged. Cici will want to get to know you better."

"And we certainly want to know this lovely young lady better. The girl who caught Jimmy's heart." Mr. Nelson grinned and winked at his wife. "Her hair is the exact same lovely color yours is."

"Was, dear, was." Mrs. Nelson smiled and, reaching up, patted his hand.

"Still every bit as lovely as ever." He bent down to kiss her cheek, and as they gazed into each other's eyes, it seemed to Jimmy as if they shared some secret.

He shook his head in wonder. After all these years, it was obvious that Blake's parents were still very much in love.

After the men had seated themselves and received cups of tea, Mr. Nelson turned to his wife. "Katie, you know Jimmy has been feeding children down by the docks. Why don't you tell him about your charitable work before the great fire?"

"All right." Her clear blue eyes shone and she smiled at Jimmy. "Let me see, now where shall I begin?"

"How about the soup kitchen?" her husband coached her.

"Soup kitchen?" Surprise rose in Jimmy. "You worked in a soup kitchen?"

She nodded and her face became serious. "You see, there were many Irish immigrants in Chicago back then. Some, like my father, were accepted and respected. But a lot of people resented the poor folk who'd come over to escape the potato famine."

"But why? Why in the world would anyone begrudge a safe harbor to people who were starving?"

She nodded. "Why indeed? You see, they came in droves, looking for employment. Many folks thought they were stealing jobs, and perhaps they were in a way, for they'd work for a pittance simply to put food on the table." She sighed. "Shantytowns popped up all over the city. Tents and shacks. The largest and most notorious was Conley's Patch. Have you ever heard of it?"

Jimmy shook his head. "Where was it?"

She looked pointedly into his eyes. "Just across the south branch of the river, by the Clark Street docks."

Jimmy inhaled sharply. "Where the tenement section is?"

She nodded. "That's right. Some of the people there are descendants of the poor Irish in Conley's Patch."

"And you did charitable work there?" Jimmy looked at the dainty matron in awe.

"Not at first. I started out working in a soup kitchen near Harrigan's. I'd go volunteer when I was off duty from the theater. I met a girl named Bridget Thornton. A very proud but desperate young woman trying to keep her family from starving." She took a sip of tea. "We became dear friends. She taught me the plight of the proud but poor people of the Patch who wanted nothing but to make a living for their families. I'll never forget my first sight of the Patch." Mrs. Nelson pressed her lips together and moisture filled her eyes. "The shanties, the tiny yards. Dirt settled everywhere. The women worked constantly keeping it out of their homes. But worse than the dirt were the ditches that ran down the center of the streets. Raw sewage, garbage, even dead animals floated down the open sewers. Sometimes a child would fall into the ditch."

"Oh yes." Mr. Nelson seemed to be reliving a memory. He shook his head and took a sip of tea.

Mrs. Nelson reached over and patted her husband on the arm, smiling into his eyes. "Sam, dear, remember when you rescued Bridget's little sister from the ditch?"

"You mean the time those little hooligans shoved her in? Oh, I remember, all right. We were both a mess. And the smell. . ." Mr. Nelson quirked his eyebrows and wrinkled his nose at the memory.

Mrs. Nelson grinned. "So I heard. But to continue, Bridget and I helped start a daycare so some of the single mothers could earn a living and married women could get jobs to supplement their husbands' incomes. Some of the women ran the daycare while others got jobs in the city."

Jimmy heard Cici give a soft sigh. He glanced her way. The smile she gave him was pinched. Unease knotted his stomach as he turned his attention back to Mrs. Nelson's story.

"Bridget and I did what we could to raise funds for the child-care center. The troupe at Harrigan's pitched in." A cloud crossed Mrs. Nelson's face. "Then the fire came."

Mr. Nelson shared a long glance with his wife. "The Patch was completely destroyed."

Jimmy could hardly imagine the devastation the poverty-stricken people must have felt. "What a tragedy. It must have been terrible for them."

"Yes," Mrs. Nelson whispered, "it was horrible. Not just for the Patch. Most of the city was destroyed or severely damaged. But my husband's father pulled the people of the city together. There was plenty of work for whoever wanted it. The people worked hard. And the city was rebuilt, including housing for the lower-income people. Instead of shanties, tenement houses were built. There were paychecks for anyone who was willing to work."

"But the people of the tenements are still poor."

Danielle sighed. "Jesus said the poor would always be with us."

"That's right." Mrs. Nelson nodded. "And just as it was

before the fire, evil men often exploited the poor, paying them unfairly low wages. And then people moved from other areas and brought their problems with them. It is true. The poor will always be with us."

"You have a heart to help people, Jimmy." Mr. Nelson smiled. "Just as my wife did and still does."

"What happened to your friend Bridget?" He wished he could take back the question as pain crossed her face.

"Bridget died a number of years ago. I kept in touch with her sister for a while. When she married and moved away, we lost contact."

Jimmy glanced at Cici. Was that impatience in her eyes? Then she smiled. Jimmy breathed with relief. She'd been disturbed by the sad story. That was all.

"Thank you for telling me about the Patch, Mrs. Nelson. And I'm very sorry you lost your friend."

He leaned back and took Cici's hand. It lay in his, cold and rigid.

&

Cici stood facing Jimmy outside the parsonage door.

"What's wrong, sweetheart?" Jimmy's concerned gaze cut through her. "You've been awfully quiet."

"Nothing. I'm fine." Tension, like a wound-up spring, threatened to burst any moment. Why did Mrs. Nelson have to tell her story? It was heartbreaking in one sense, but it also showed what a few people could do if they cared enough. Cici hated the feelings the stories had created in her. And she was pretty sure they'd had a strong effect on Jimmy.

"Are you sure?" His brow furrowed and he tucked a loose curl behind her ear.

"No! No, Jimmy, I'm not sure. In fact, I'm quite sure I'm not fine." She jerked away from him.

A startled look crossed his face. "Honey, what is it? Why are you so upset?"

"I need to know, Jimmy. Have you made a decision about law

school? I assumed you had, but you never really said for sure."

He looked away then faced her again. "Let's sit on the swing for a little while."

With dread pounding at her, she sat beside him.

He took her hand and gazed into her eyes. "Cici, if I should decide not to, will you still marry me? Do you care for me enough to be the wife of a missionary?"

Her mouth quivered, and before she could stop them, tears began to roll from her eyes and down her cheeks. "So you've made your decision?"

"I didn't say that, Cici." He ran his thumb across her cheeks, wiping the tears away. "But I need to know if you'll marry me either way."

"I don't know."

Resignation crossed his face.

She felt as though a knife had pierced her heart. "I love you. I promise I do. But I don't know if I can be a missionary's wife, Jimmy."

"But honey, it's not like we'd be going far away. We'd be right here near those we love and. . .this is about doing what Jesus would want us to do."

"And you believe He wants you to be a missionary to the poor."

He took a deep breath and ran his hand through his hair. "I thought so. I'm not sure anymore. I'm confused, Cici. And I don't like it."

"It's because of me, isn't it? It's my fault you don't know what you're supposed to do."

"No, of course not."

"I think it is. I'll try not to influence you, Jimmy. I have to think now. I love you." Jumping up, she ran to the door, pushed her way through, and slammed it behind her.

≈

God, help me. Help me to at least give it a try.

Cici's lips trembled and she pressed them together and

forced a smile as Danielle opened the door of her home. "Hello. I hope I'm not late for the meeting."

"Not at all. You are just in time. We're about to begin." With a big smile, Danielle motioned for her to come in. "I'm glad you decided to come."

About twenty women crowded the parlor. Blake's mother waved from across the room, and a woman sitting on a sofa moved over and made room for Cici. "Aren't you Rev. Willow's daughter?"

"Yes, ma'am." Cici sat by the woman and smiled.

"Everyone, I'd like for you to meet Cici Willow." Danielle looked around the room. "I believe her mother has agreed to be a part of our group as well but had other duties to fulfill today. Now if we could call the meeting to order. I believe Mary Baker has some news about a building."

"Yes indeed." A younger woman stood. "An empty church building, as a matter of fact. It has been abandoned for so long the owners were quite willing to let us use it free of charge. We will, of course, be responsible for the upkeep. There is no gaslight or electricity, so we'll need to gather up lamps and kerosene to take over."

Several women offered lamps. Danielle counted and wrote down the names.

"Are there any tables?" another woman asked.

"Yes, that's the good thing. All their Sunday school tables are still there." She grinned. "And even better, there's a stove, so we won't have to cook the soup elsewhere and transport it there."

"We'll need to find someone to bring wood," Danielle said.

"I think my father-in-law might be willing to do that. I'll ask," Mrs. Baker said.

Plans were made about who would bring what ingredients.

"Now about the food baskets. . ." Danielle tapped a pencil against her chair.

"A man who owns a box company goes to our church."

Cici was happy to be able to make a contribution to the conversation. "He always gives away the imperfect ones that he can't sell. They would work very well as containers for the groceries. Would you like me to check with him?"

"That would be wonderful, Cici." Danielle smiled and made a notation.

"Oh, and one more thing." Cici leaned forward. "My mother wanted me to extend an offer on behalf of her sewing circle to make socks and hats for you to include with the baskets."

Murmurs and nods went around the room.

"That would be grand." Mrs. Nelson smiled. "Winter will be here before we know it. Please extend our thanks to your mother and the ladies of her sewing circle."

Warmth enveloped Cici as she returned the smile and nodded.

For an hour they planned; then they agreed to get together again on Tuesday.

Cici felt more peace as she rode home on the streetcar than she had since the dinner on Sunday. Maybe if Jimmy really did become a missionary, she could handle it. At least by getting involved with this project to help the people in the tenements, she'd find out.

fifteen

An icy chill ran up Jimmy's spine as he spotted Cobb and Sutton through the dusty window. He took a step back into the darkness then cautiously peered in once more.

They sat at a table in the far corner, laughing. Cobb turned up his mug and took a long swig of coffee.

Nausea hit Jimmy and he closed his eyes. Cobb, his friend, he'd thought. Could he have just run into Sutton? Maybe he was getting information for Jimmy. But reason told him otherwise.

Sutton stood and threw some coins on the table, said something, and headed for the door.

Jimmy ducked around the corner of the building until he heard the man's footsteps walking off down the sidewalk. Anger rose in him. More at himself than at Cobb. He should have known better. Cobb had been Sutton's main boy for years before Jimmy and Danni had fallen into their lives. He peered into the window once more.

Cobb stood and sauntered across the café. The door swung open. Cobb stood there, a look of shock on his face. "Hey, Jimbo."

"Hi, Cobb, old friend." He made no attempt to keep the anger from resonating from his voice. Cobb would know right away he'd seen them.

"You were right, Jimbo. I just ran into Sutton. Matter of fact, you just missed him."

"Yeah, I know." Jimmy narrowed his eyes. "What's the big idea, Cobb?"

"What do you mean? I told you. . ." He stopped and shook his head. "Oh, what's the use? All right, I knew Sutton was out."

"Why'd you lie to me? We're supposed to be friends."

Cobb huffed out a loud breath of air. "I didn't figure you'd believe me that Sutton's changed, that's why."

Jimmy laughed. "Changed? Sutton? Okay, Cobb, how's he changed? Does he have a new type of crime ring going this time?"

"No, Jimmy, listen. He really has changed. You should hear him talk." Cobb's eyes were bright as he grabbed Jimmy's shoulders. "He wants to help the people around here. Just like you do. He was happy when I told him what you were up to."

Jimmy jerked away. "You really believe that, don't you? Wake up. Sutton is the same rotten crook he's always been."

"Well, that's a fine Christian way to talk." Cobb's face twisted and he narrowed his eyes. "Don't give the man a chance. Just take it for granted he can't change. And to think I'd almost decided maybe you were right about the God stuff. I was even thinking about going to church with you."

Uncertainty wormed its way into Jimmy's mind; then immediately he pushed it away. "Cici and I ran into Sutton at the theater. He hasn't changed. He practically threatened Danni."

"Why? What did he say?"

"He said. . . Well, it wasn't so much what he said as the way he said it and the look he gave me when he said it." He narrowed his eyes. "Believe me. He's up to no good. At least where Danni and I are concerned."

"Aw, come on, Jimbo. Can't you admit you might be wrong? Give Sutton a chance. He wants to talk to you."

"Sorry. Let him fool you if you want to, but I'm not having anything to do with him."

"Okay, have it your way." Cobb swung around and started down the sidewalk, then turned and faced Jimmy. "But Sutton's a changed man, Jimbo. You're gonna see." Cobb stalked off down the street.

Jimmy sighed. Could Cobb be right? He turned and headed toward Clark Street and the streetcar line. No, Sutton was the same. He only hoped Cobb would see that before he got himself into trouble.

When Jimmy got home, he found Danni and Blake in the parlor. He dropped into a chair.

"Is something wrong?" Danni threw him a worried look. "It's not Cici, is it?"

He inhaled and let the air out with a *whoosh*. "No, I went to the tenements to take some medicine to Mike. He's been sick."

"Oh, how is he?"

"He'll be okay. But I saw Cobb with Sutton." He relayed the conversation they'd had.

Danielle frowned. "Is it possible? Anyone can change, you know. Maybe Sutton found Jesus while he was in prison."

"I don't think so, Danni." He hadn't had a chance to tell Blake about his encounter with Sutton, as he'd intended. But Danielle had begun to go about alone again. They both needed to know. "I ran into Sutton while I was leaving the theater the other night."

Danni's hand trembled as she laid it on Blake's.

He put an arm around her and drew her close. "What happened?"

"Well, he seemed threatening to me. But I may have been mistaken." He went ahead and relayed the conversation word for word, describing Sutton's attitude and expressions as well as possible.

Blake's lips were tight. "Danielle, you need to stay near the house again."

She jumped up and stomped her foot as her face crumpled. "I won't let that man run my life. I'm not afraid of him."

"Sweetheart, please." Blake drew her down beside him again.

Jimmy's heart felt like it would tear in two at his sister's anguish. "Danni, please, just for a little while. Let me watch him for a while."

"We'll do better than that." Anger tightened Blake's face. "I'll put a private detective on his tail. If he goes near her, the police will be there before he can make a move."

"Well then, I won't need to stay inside." The hope in her eyes clutched at Jimmy and he glanced at Blake.

"No, sweetheart." Blake brought her hand up to his lips and kissed it. "You don't want to take chances. Please stay inside until we know what he's up to."

"But what about the soup kitchen and food baskets?" Despair filled her voice.

"There are twenty or more women involved with it, Danni." Jimmy's reminder only brought a frown his way. "They can get by without you for a while."

She sighed. "Very well. But this can't go on forever. I won't remain a prisoner in my own home."

Jimmy thought of her words as he went up to his room. He intended to do everything in his power to make sure she wouldn't be.

 za

The smell of cabbage and tomatoes assaulted Cici's nostrils as she dipped soup from the large pot and filled another bowl. She handed it to an old woman who flashed a toothless grin and walked away. Cici stretched her back and looked toward the door. The line ran down the street as far as she could see. How could there be so many hungry people in this one neighborhood alone?

"Cici, dear," Mrs. Baker called from the end of the food line, "could you get some bread out of the other room, please?"

"Yes, ma'am." She gladly turned the soup ladle over to a woman walking by and headed for the back room. The smell of yeast wafted up from the stacks of long loaves of bread that stood on the table by the open window. She grabbed four loaves and carried them back to where Mrs. Baker stood with a sharp knife. "Would you like me to help slice?" She swiped the back of her arm across her damp forehead.

"No. Why don't you relieve Dottie? She's been standing over that cauldron for an hour now."

"Yes, ma'am." She headed back to the kitchen and took over for the hefty woman who stood moving a big wooden spoon around the enormous pot.

"Be sure to keep stirring so it doesn't stick." The woman handed her the big wooden spoon and stepped over to the water barrel.

She did as she was told for another hour, dizzy from the overwhelming smell of cabbage, onions, and tomatoes swimming in beef broth until the last pot had been removed to the serving line. Cici grabbed a tin cup and filled it with water. She drank it all then went to relieve someone on the food line.

With so many of the women taking care of the food boxes, a handful of them were kept busy dishing up the food.

"Here, Martha, let me take over here. Go get yourself a cool drink."

With a grateful look, the young girl relinquished her place by one of the soup pots.

Cici picked up the ladle. She scooped soup into a bowl and looked up.

A small boy, not more than six or seven, stood staring at her with rounded blue eyes. The hunger in those eyes nearly made her heart stop. She handed him the bowl, and when his hands wrapped around it, he grinned. "You sure are purty, miss."

She smiled as warmth enveloped her heart. "Why, thank you. You're pretty handsome yourself."

Red washed over his face and he grinned again. A tiny girl who followed with her mother giggled. The boy moved on down the line and the little girl peered up at her.

Cici smiled. "Yes, you're mighty pretty, too." She filled two bowls of soup and smiled at the mother. "Do you need help carrying these?"

"Oh no, Patsy can carry hers." She turned to the child. "Be careful now, honey."

Cici watched them as she filled another bowl. She breathed a sigh of relief when the little girl set her bowl safely on the table then ran back to where the bread was being handed out.

The door opened and a boy hobbled in on one crutch. He glanced around as though looking for someone then came to the line. He eyed the soup as though he hadn't eaten in days. Mrs. Nelson filled a bowl for him and he started toward a table.

Suddenly the door flew open. A red-faced man stomped in. He looked around and with thunder in his eyes headed for the lame boy. He jerked the bowl from his hand and set it on the nearest table. With his jaw clenched, he spoke quietly.

The boy nodded and followed him out of the room.

"Why did he do that?" Pain pierced Cici's heart, and she wiped at the tears that gushed from her eyes. "The boy was hungry."

The woman who stood in front of her shook her head. "Hiram Jones is a proud man. Won't take no handouts."

"But. . ." Cici could find no words. Nausea clutched her stomach.

The woman reached over and took the bowl from her hand. She smiled at Cici. "Don't worry, honey. Hiram makes sure that boy has his supper ever' day. He may be a little hollow, but he ain't starvin'."

Cici stared as the woman took her bowl and went down the line to get her bread. How could she be so uncaring? The boy was lame. And he was hungry. And how could a father be so cruel? A shiver ran over Cici. She couldn't stand this. She started to untie her apron.

A young girl, maybe thirteen or fourteen, faced her with lowered eyes.

Cici sighed and dropped her arms. She filled a bowl and held it out. "Here you go."

The girl raised her brown eyes and reached for the bowl. "Thank you, miss," she whispered.

Well, okay, she'd stay until everyone had soup. And she'd help clean up. But she wouldn't come back. Ever.

❧

The coolness of the foyer greeted Cici as she walked into the parsonage. She stood for a moment just inside the door and inhaled the smell of the furniture oil that made the hall tables shine. She breathed a sigh of relief. She'd thought the smell of cabbage and unwashed bodies would remain in her nostrils forever, but as she stood there, the familiar home smells took over.

"Cici, dear, why are you standing there?" Her mother stood in the doorway, a concerned smile on her face.

Should she tell her? No, Mama was so strong. What would she think of her daughter being so weak that she would give up her charitable work after one day? "I'm just tired, Mama. I think I'll go up and change. Do you need my help with anything?"

"No, not for an hour or so. Is Jimmy coming over tonight?"

"No, ma'am. Not tonight." She started up the stairs. "Oh, Jimmy, I tried. I truly did."

sixteen

Jimmy took a bite of ham and one of cheese then followed with a hunk of rye bread. He glanced sideways at Cobb who was peering up and down the street. Jimmy grinned. "What are you looking for?" As if he didn't know.

"Where are all the kids?" Confusion crossed his face. Lately, to Jimmy's satisfaction, Cobb had been sharing his lunch with the hungry children, too.

"The soup kitchen. Haven't you heard about it?"

"Yeah, of course I've heard of it. Everyone's heard of it. But I thought. . ."

"What?"

"I thought the kids would still come."

Jimmy smiled at the look of disappointment on Cobb's face. "They'll be here later. I always tell them a story after work."

"Yeah? I guess I missed out on what's been going on while I was out with the *Eastland*."

"Guess so."

Cobb cleared his throat. "Hey, Jimbo, I got something to tell you."

"Yeah? What is it?" Probably one of his corny jokes.

"It's about Sutton." He picked nervously at the paper around his sandwich.

Jimmy stiffened. "Cobb, I don't want to hear anything about how Sutton has changed."

"No." He took a deep breath. "You were right, Jimbo."

Alert to the tension in Cobb's voice, Jimmy put his food back in the bucket. "What is it? What do you know?"

"I'm not sure. But Sutton's been making remarks lately. Nothing I can really put my finger on." His brow furrowed. "Jimbo, I think he's planning some kind of revenge on you and Danni."

Jimmy's voice rose as he stared at Cobb. "What kind of revenge?"

"I don't know. I promise I don't. It's more a feeling than anything else. The way he looks when he mentions Danni. And you, too." He took a swig of water from his canteen. "Be careful, and tell that husband of Danni's to watch out. Sutton hates him."

Jimmy took a deep breath. "Thanks, Cobb. I know it isn't easy for you to go against Sutton."

"It isn't. He's been like a father to me."

Jimmy shook his head. "Cobb, a father doesn't teach his kids to steal for him. He was using you the same as he was using the rest of us."

Cobb sighed. "Yeah, I guess I know that now. He's been hinting around for me to do a job for him. I've dodged the idea though."

Jimmy nodded. He hoped Cobb would continue to hold out. Sutton was ruthless and wouldn't bat an eye if Cobb went back to prison.

"I'm sorry for the way I acted, Jimbo. I should have believed you. Guess I did, really, but didn't want to admit it."

"It's okay. I understand." It was hard to face the fact someone you cared about wasn't what you thought. Jimmy's stomach clenched. He only hoped that wasn't the way it was with him and Cici. But she was helping out at the food kitchen. So that proved she had a heart for the people. . .didn't it?

"I've been thinking." Cobb scratched his head. "Maybe I'll go to that church with you next Sunday."

Jimmy laughed and clapped Cobb on the shoulder. "That's great. I've been praying you would. You won't be sorry, Cobb."

Cobb grinned. "I hope God don't faint when I walk in."

Jimmy winced then grinned. Cobb didn't mean any disrespect. "You don't need to worry about that, buddy. God's a lot stronger than that." Jimmy wrote down the directions to the church and promised to be waiting on the steps for Cobb.

They finished their lunch and went back to work unloading a cargo ship. They seldom had the chance to work together since the *Eastland* was so busy.

Jimmy was surprised when Cobb followed him to where the children were waiting.

They were both surrounded the moment they seated themselves.

Little Mike peered up into Cobb's face. "You going ta tell us stories, too?"

"Naw. We better all listen to Jimmy." Cobb grinned at the boy and rubbed his shock of greasy hair.

After everyone was settled, Jimmy looked around. "Okay. How many of you went to church last week?"

One little hand went up. Maria Consuela. "I did, Jimmy. I like church."

"That's good, Maria." He glanced around. "Anyone else?"

Looking everywhere but at Jimmy, the children managed to avoid answering.

Jimmy sighed. "Okay, but you know I told you my stories don't take the place of the house of God. Remember?"

"I'll go next week, Jimmy," Bridget piped up. "I promise. And I'll take Patrick and Mike, too."

"Good girl, Bridget. You can tell me all about it next Monday, okay?"

She nodded and gave a nervous laugh.

Jimmy hoped she wouldn't back out. Maybe he should offer to take some of the children with him on Sunday. Something to think about. Silence fell as he told them the story of a boy named Samuel who lived in the temple and heard the voice of God.

"Hows come I can't hear the voice of God, Jimmy?" Little

Sally, always wanting to know and never afraid to ask, peered up at him.

How could he answer in a way she'd understand? "You can hear Him, Sally." He placed his hand on the front of her torn dress. "Right here, in your heart."

She looked down. "How?"

Jimmy groaned. *Help me, Lord.* He smiled into the little girl's innocent blue eyes. "Hmm. Well, let's see now. Do you ever think about doing something naughty and then something tells you not to?"

She nodded. "Mama says it's my konchunch."

"Yes, your mama is right. God talks to us sometimes through our consciences." Okay, but that wasn't enough. He could see in her eyes that it wasn't. "And He also talks to us through the Bible. Did you know that?"

"Mama has a Bible. Sometimes she reads it to me." She scrunched up her face. "But I can't unnerstan' it."

"You will, Sally, when you get a little older." What now? *Help me, Lord.* He took a deep breath and smiled. "But that's not the only way God talks to us, Sally. Do you ever want to tell your mama thank you when she's worked hard to do something nice for you?"

"Like when she makes sweet johnnycakes?" Her mouth puckered into a little pink bow. "Is it God that tells me to give her a hug?"

"That's exactly right, Bridget."

She rubbed her dress in the spot over her heart and her eyes lit up. "Oh, I know now. God talks to me lots of times. You know what, Jimmy?"

"What, sweetheart?"

She smiled and held out her arms. "I think God's telling me to give you a hug, too."

æ

"Mama." Cici bit her lip as she folded the turnover dough over the apple filling.

"Yes, dear?" She straightened with the pan of cookies she'd removed from the oven. Smiling, she set them on a towel on the counter.

"How do you keep it up? I mean, all your responsibilities as a minister's wife must be overwhelming."

Mama stared. "Whatever do you mean? Of course I'm busy. But most wives and mothers are."

"But it's different with you, Mama. Everyone depends on you for everything." Cici frowned and threw both hands up, inadvertently slinging flour in the air. "Oh, I'm sorry. I'll clean it up."

"Wait, Cecilia. Let's sit a minute." She pulled out a chair at the table and Cici followed suit. "Now, why don't you tell me what this is all about?"

Cici sighed. "I'm pretty sure Jimmy will decide to give up law to be a missionary."

"I see. And you don't like the idea?" She picked a piece of lint from her apron and stuffed it in the pocket.

"Well, of course I want him to follow his heart." She sighed again. "I'm not sure, though, if I should marry him."

"But you're in love with him, aren't you?"

"Yes, but I don't know if I can be a minister's wife, Mama." She ducked her head, avoiding her mother's eyes.

"But darling, if you love him, does it matter which direction he chooses to go?" Her brows furrowed. "Isn't it a woman's place to conform to her husband's choices?"

"Yes, which is why I'm not sure if I should marry him."

"I'm not sure I understand, Cecilia. Does my life seem so bad to you?"

Cici groaned inwardly. Why couldn't she be more like this wonderful woman? "Mama"—she reached over and placed her hand on her mother's work-worn one—"I've watched you stay home night after night while Papa took care of other people. And I know it was his duty, but I saw how lonely you were. And you've dropped everything at a moment's notice to go cook and clean for someone who was ill."

"But any Christian would have done the same." She slipped her hand from beneath Cici's and lifted it to Cici's cheek. "You would have done the same."

"Once in a while, perhaps, but it's constant. Every time people have needs, they run to you and Papa." Perhaps she shouldn't have begun this conversation. She was only making herself sound selfish and uncaring.

"This is what God has called us to, daughter. Surely you know that. When I married your father, I answered his call as well."

"Maybe that's the answer." Cici frowned. "Maybe God isn't calling me to the same thing he's calling Jimmy to."

"Perhaps not. That's something you need to find out for sure before you marry him."

"How do you stand all the sacrifices you have to make?" The words shot out like a cannonball from a cannon. Cici covered her mouth with her fingers. "Oh, Mama, I'm sorry. I didn't mean to shout."

"Cecilia, I have never considered anything I've done for God and His people to be a sacrifice. To me, it has always been a work of love."

Cici stared at her mother's serene face for a moment. She meant it. This was true love. Her mother's love for her God and her husband. Oh, how she wished she could be like that. Why wasn't she? She'd been raised by God-fearing, wonderful parents who had taught her all about the love of Christ. And they hadn't just taught her with words. They'd taught her with their own lives. What was wrong with her that she wasn't like them?

"Cecilia, is there something else you're not telling me?" Worry sounded in her voice.

"Oh, Mama, I don't know how you stand to see people hurting all the time. And some people are so mean. How do you deal with them?"

"Did something happen at the soup kitchen?" Mama took her hand and looked into her eyes. "Something did happen. Tell me."

Starting at the beginning, Cici let it pour out. The hungry children, the mothers trying to keep starvation from the door, the lame boy and his angry father. Finally, she burst into tears. "I know I can't stand it, Mama. How can I help people when I'm so weak?"

"Oh, honey, of course it's difficult when you come face-to-face with the hard side of life." She pulled Cici's head over against her shoulder and smoothed her hair. "Perhaps I was wrong to shelter you so."

"No, Mama, you weren't wrong." She took a deep breath and forced a smile. "We'd best finish the baking so we can get started on supper."

Her mother smiled, but worry shadowed her eyes. "You're right. We wouldn't want your papa's supper to be late." She faced Cici. "You need to take all these concerns to God. He's the only One who can give you the answers."

Cici nodded and went to get the broom to clean the flour off the floor. Maybe if she tried harder, she could change. That was it. She hadn't planned to go help out at the soup kitchen anymore, but she'd force herself to go. After all, if God saw she was trying, He'd help her. Wouldn't He? And who knew? Maybe Jimmy would decide to go back to law school after all.

❧

Blake stood and paced the study. "And Cobb said it was an impression he got? He couldn't give you anything specific to go on?"

"No." Jimmy shook his head. "But Cobb's not one to imagine things. And Sutton's been like an idol to him. If he thinks Sutton's up to something, I believe him."

Blake nodded and leaned against his desk. "I've got a man following him. He hasn't reported anything suspicious yet.

We'll have to keep our eyes open, too. I'm thinking about working at home until this is settled."

"Good idea. I'd feel a lot better knowing you were here. What about your appointments?"

"I'm sure Dad won't mind taking them. Or we can assign them to someone else. If anyone insists on seeing me personally, he or she will have to wait." He sat behind his desk and leaned back. "I'm thinking of paying a personal visit to Sutton."

Startled, Jimmy stood and leaned over the desk. "Don't do that, Blake. First of all, we're not sure where he's staying. And second, you know what he's capable of. You need to stay here and take care of Danni."

Blake tossed him a side grin. "Okay. I won't do anything stupid. But I suggest you don't either."

"It's a deal. Let's wait for Cobb or the detective to get more information then go from there. In the meantime, we'll keep Danni safe."

Blake sighed and stood. "I'd better tell her."

Jimmy gave him a look of sympathy, glad he wasn't the one who had to impart the disturbing news to his sister.

Lord, protect Danni. Don't let that man get his hands on her.

As worried as Jimmy was about Danni, he could only imagine how hard it must be on Blake to know the man had evil plans against his wife.

seventeen

The fishy smell permeating the building wasn't bad at all. Cici chuckled as she stirred the pot of chowder. Amazing how quickly one could get accustomed to things. And to think, just a couple of weeks ago, she was ready to run away in hopeless tears.

A tap on the back window drew her attention and she grabbed a tin bowl from the shelf and filled it to the brim with the soup. She headed toward the window, snatching up a slab of bread she'd cut ahead of time.

Larry grinned and propped his crutch against the building so he could take the food she passed through the window. "Thanks, Miss Cici."

"You are very welcome, Larry. Just leave the bowl and spoon on the window ledge when you're finished." She tousled his head and headed back to the stove.

"Cici, we need a refill." Mrs. Baker's granddaughter, Nancy, set an empty pot on the table beside the stove.

"All right. This is ready. I'll help you carry." She tossed the girl a thick rag and, with another, grabbed the handle on one side of the pot. Together they managed to carry it to the food line.

"Thank you, girls." Mrs. Nelson smiled and motioned to the short line that scarcely reached the door. "Don't bother to make another pot. This should be plenty."

"Do you want me to start kitchen cleanup?"

"If you'll take over here, I'll do that. I need a change." Blake's mother wiped her sleeve across her face and stepped back from the long counter.

"That's fine with me." Cici took her place, noticing that a mother with four children stood waiting.

Cici smiled at her. "Why don't you find a table for you and your family? We'll bring your food over."

"Thank you kindly." With a smile of relief, the woman guided her children to a corner table.

Cici started filling bowls then turned her head at a tap on her shoulder.

Nancy stood behind her. "I can carry two at a time while you fill the rest."

"Oh good." She handed two filled bowls to the girl, then grabbed two more bowls and spooned the chowder into them. Nancy was back by the time they were filled.

"Here, if you'll take these, I'll take the last bowl and some bread."

A tiny girl with wild blond curls grinned at her as she set a bowl in front of her. "You have hair just like mine."

"Well, so I do." Cici wrinkled her nose and grinned back at the child.

"My name's Sally. What's yours?"

"Cecilia. But my friends call me Cici."

"Am I your friend?" The little girl's round blue eyes waited.

"I would like very much for you to be my friend." Cici held out her hand and Sally grasped it with her tiny one and gave a hearty shake.

"Whew. You have a strong handshake." Cici shook her hand, pretending to be in pain.

Sally giggled.

A boy across from her snorted. "Aw, that ain't strong. Here, feel mine." He stuck his dirty hand across the table.

Cici forced herself not to cringe, took a deep breath, and reached for his hand. "Now don't hurt me. I'm not too strong."

"Okay, I'll try not to." He gave her a firm shake.

"I think he's right, Sally. His handshake is stronger than

yours or mine." She rubbed her hands together.

"Yeah, but he's not as strong as my friend Jimmy." She frowned at her brother.

"Aw, Jimmy's a grown-up. And besides, he ain't just *your* friend."

"Is, too."

"Is not."

Maybe she'd better try to break this up. She smiled at the mother who was spooning soup into her toddler's mouth. The mother shook her head and smiled back. "You kids get to eating and stop bothering Miss Cici."

Cici laughed. "They aren't bothering me. But I do need to get back to work." She waved at the children and went back to the food line.

"The children seem to like you, Cici." Mrs. Baker placed bread on a plate and handed it across to an old man whose trembling hand tried to steady a bowl of soup.

"Here, let me help." Cici took the bowl and plate and walked beside him to a chair at one of the tables. He seated himself and began to eat, ignoring her. But after all, she wasn't doing this for thanks.

Warmth flooded over her as she continued serving the nourishing soup. She wasn't sure what had changed her, but there was no doubt she was changing. She was able to have contact with the people without falling apart. And she was learning to do what she could and leave the rest in God's hands. Could it be that He had answered her prayer to help her change? It must be.

But what was she to do about Gail? She was supposed to meet her at the café tomorrow. But she didn't want to meet her. She sighed. She'd have to see her one more time and let her know. That would be the polite thing to do.

❧

The early summer foliage brightened the park with greens, yellows, and pinks, with an occasional blue or red scattered about. Jimmy smiled as Cici stepped around a patch of wildflowers so she wouldn't crush them. Her face was radiant today and a burst of hope penetrated the doubt that Jimmy had carried around lately. Maybe the work she'd been doing at the soup kitchen had helped her to see ministering to the people in a different light.

"Oh, here's a good spot, Jimmy." She turned toward a wrought iron bench that stood beneath a silver maple. "I love to hear the leaves rustle, don't you?"

Jimmy would have loved to hear a steamroller today as long as Cici was smiling and happy. "Yes, my favorite tree." He sat beside her and took her hand.

"Now, Jimmy. Don't do that. Someone will see." But her hand remained in his and she smiled up at him. She leaned back and sighed. "I'm so glad we had this Sunday afternoon free. I love our families and friends, but this is better."

Jimmy inhaled sharply. This was good. All right—this was very, very good. "I feel the same way." Maybe he should wait until another time to tell her. No, that would be cowardly and unfair. She had a right to know. She had a right to decide what she wanted to do. "Cici." He rubbed his thumb across her ring, praying she wouldn't fling it at him. "Honey, I've made my decision."

Only a slight tightening of her hand revealed that she'd heard him. She bit her lip. "All right, Jimmy. It's good that you know what you're supposed to do. I know the indecision has been difficult for you."

"And for you as well." An almost imperceptible nod of her head answered her agreement.

"There's something I need to tell you, Cici. Something that might help you to understand. I should have told you before." But how he hated to speak of the subject.

"All right, Jimmy. I'm listening." She squeezed his hand.

"When I was four years old, my father died at sea. Mother, having no means of support, went to work cooking and cleaning in a boardinghouse. At least I think that's what it was. A few months later, she died in childbirth."

At her gasp, he paused for a moment.

"Danni was ten. The next morning, the woman who owned the place turned us out on the street with nothing but our few articles of clothing."

"Oh, Jimmy, how awful." Cici eyes filled and she blinked rapidly and squeezed Jimmy's arm. "But what did you do?"

"We wandered the streets all morning, in the cold October wind, hungry, as we'd had only a bite or two of bread since the day before." A shiver ran over his skin at the memory. "We walked to the docks and hid behind a large crate to get out of the wind for a while. We didn't know what to do, because we'd always had our mother to take care of us. Anyway, due to a series of events, we wound up at the home of a man who ran a child crime ring."

"No. How terrible." Her voice trembled.

Jimmy squeezed her hand. "Of course, we didn't know he was a criminal at the time. All we knew was that the house was warm and he gave us hot soup and bread. And a cot to sleep on."

He ran his hand over his eyes and took a deep breath. "For some reason, he took a liking to us and didn't send us out to steal the way the other children did. At that time, my leg was lame. That's probably why he didn't send me out. And later, we found he had other things in mind for my sister. Thank God, we were rescued before his plans were fulfilled."

Cici nodded. "I think I understand now why you have a heart for the poor. Especially the children."

"Yes, that was it in the beginning. But God has shown me His plan, sweetheart. With my compassion for the people and my connection with people of means, there is much I can do to help." He tilted her chin up and looked into her eyes. "Cici, I intend to enter seminary in September. I've already spoken to your father, and he is making arrangements for me to meet with the dean of his old school."

She nodded. "How will we live?"

Jimmy inhaled sharply. Had she said *we*? He gazed at her questioningly.

A smile started in the blue depths of her eyes and then tipped her pink lips. "We do have to live, you know."

He pulled her close and she gave a contented sigh. "I was so afraid of losing you."

"I was afraid, too, Jimmy. I didn't know what was wrong with me. I had a dread and a terrible fear. And not only that—I wanted excitement." Suddenly she grew very still. "Jimmy, where is that terrible man?"

"He was sent to prison, but he's out now. In fact, you saw him that night we were leaving the theater." He sighed. "And I'm afraid he's up to no good again. He may even have plans to harm Danni."

She took a deep breath. "What happened to the children?"

"Some of the older boys were sentenced to jail. The younger ones were placed in a children's home. "But what's wrong? You're so pale."

She shook her head. "Was Danni the only girl?"

"No, there were two others. Both about my age."

Her face crumpled. "Jimmy, there's something I need to tell you. I don't want to, but you have a right to know. After you hear, you may not want to marry me." She pulled away, and once more her eyes filled with tears.

Startled, Jimmy tried to draw her close again but she resisted. "Cici, what is it? There's nothing you could tell me that would change my mind about marrying you."

"Not now. There's one more thing I must do. Then I'll tell you. If you still want to marry me afterwards, I will joyfully become your wife and share your ministry."

❧

That swine. That monster. Sutton. Cici nearly gagged at the thought of him. And to think she had thought he was a gentleman. Cici shoved through the door at Tony's Place. After the bright sunlight, it was dark and almost frightening. Strange, she'd never noticed that before. She stood inside the door for a moment, letting her eyes adjust.

Gail, at her usual table, waved when she saw Cici walking toward her.

Cici seated herself across from Gail and looked at her silently. Her heart thumped so hard her chest hurt.

A startled look crossed Gail's face. "What's wrong?"

"You tell me, Gail. What is wrong?" She clenched her fist and narrowed her eyes at the girl she'd thought was her friend.

Gail gave a nervous laugh. "I don't know what you're talking about."

"Tell me again how you know Sutton. A friend of your family, you say?"

"That's right." A guarded shadow filled her eyes.

"Your family being. . . ?"

"What?"

"Tell me about your family, Gail. And tell me exactly what part Sutton plays in it."

"Cici, listen—"

"No, you listen. I know all about your little family of criminals. Sutton being the father criminal of them all."

Gail's eyes darted around the café. "Keep your voice down. All right. I don't know how you found out, but yeah, it's true. I was part of his gang from the time I was six. I would have starved to death otherwise. But I couldn't expect you to understand that. You with your oh-so-prissy upbringing. And look at you now. I didn't know any better and couldn't do any better. But you've turned your back on a family who loves you. Why do you think you're any better than me?"

"That's right. I did turn my back on everything I knew to be right. But as for your not knowing any better, what about now, Gail? You pretended to be my friend to set me up for

Sutton. And what was that all about, I'd like to know?"

Gail's face had tightened. "I don't know what you're talking about."

"I want to talk to him." She would find out what he was plotting against Danni and Jimmy. Whatever it was, she'd find out and tell Jimmy so he could stop him.

"But why? I don't understand what has you so riled up. Sutton's not breaking the law anymore."

"Just tell me how to get in touch with him."

"He's out of town."

"Send him a message."

"I don't know where he is, Cici. Honest." A light appeared in her eye. "But I know where he'll be on Saturday morning."

"All right, tell me."

"I'm supposed to meet him on board the *Eastland* around seven Saturday morning." A look of cunning crossed her face. "In fact, he asked me to bring you, too. Some big shot invited him to this big company picnic. They're going to Michigan City, Indiana. There's supposed to be a talent scout on board."

"I don't care anything about a talent scout. But I am going to talk to Sutton one way or the other. Where should I meet you?"

"On board, I guess."

"So you can talk to Sutton before I get there? No, I'll meet you first."

"All right. Meet me on the dock." She smiled. "I won't tell him anything, Cici. I promise."

Without saying good-bye, Cici jumped up and left. Gail was up to something. But what could happen on a ship with a crowd of people around?

eighteen

Jimmy tapped on the chapel door and waited, the hot July sun boring into the top of his head. Slow footsteps approached the door. That didn't sound like Paul's quick step.

The door swung open. The pastor's wife, Anne, faced him, her eyes weary. "Mr. Grayson, please come in."

"I don't wish to intrude. Would it be possible for me to see the pastor?" Something didn't feel right. She wasn't her usual friendly self.

"My husband has been ill. He's still not well. But I'm sure he will see you. If you'll be seated, I'll go ask."

"Perhaps I should come back when he's fully recovered. I don't want to intrude if he's not feeling well."

"No, no. He is feeling some better today and will probably be happy to have someone besides me to talk to." She smiled weakly and turned to go.

A twinge of worry bit at Jimmy. If Paul was better, why was his usually cheerful wife so downcast?

In a moment, she was back. "He's eager to see you, Mr. Grayson. Please come on up."

Jimmy followed her up the narrow stairs to the small but clean and cozy apartment.

She led him down a short hallway and held a door, motioning him in, then turned and left.

Paul sat beside an open window, his Bible on his lap. "Jimmy, I'm so glad to see you. Please come in and visit awhile."

Jimmy shook the pastor's hand and sat in a small over-stuffed chair facing him. "I'm sorry to hear you've been ill."

Jimmy peered at Paul's face.

The pastor's normally tanned skin had faded to a sickly yellow. "But I'm better now." He smiled. "I'm glad you came over, Jimmy. I wasn't sure I'd get to see you again before we leave."

"You're going away?" He hoped not for long. Jimmy had come to depend on the man's friendship.

"I'm afraid so." He took a sip from a glass of water on the table. "You see, I seem to have some sort of lung condition. Nothing fatal or contagious, but it appears to sap my strength. The doctor insists that we take an extended vacation in a dry area." He sighed.

"For how long?" Surely he'd be back.

Paul shrugged. "He doesn't seem to think I should return to this area. I've informed my headquarters that I'll be requesting a church in a drier climate when I'm able to perform my duties."

"I'm so sorry, Paul. I'll miss you."

"We'll keep in touch. After all, there's always the post." He smiled. "Now, what's on your mind, my friend? You must have had a reason for coming out in this heat."

Jimmy shook his head. "I wanted you to know I've decided to enroll in seminary in the fall. Rev. Willow put me in contact with his old administrator there."

"That is wonderful news. Jimmy, I'm so happy to hear that. And especially glad you'll be attending the school I graduated from. I've been praying for guidance for you since you told me what was in your heart."

"Yes. If I can be half the spiritual leader you are, I'll be content."

"Jimmy, have you ever thought of pastoring a church?"

"The thought has crossed my mind. But of course, you are the—" He stopped and realization dawned as Paul grinned. "Oh no, I could never take your place."

"Then don't try. Take your own place. I'm sure with

recommendations from Rev. Willow and myself, you could fill the position here."

"But I haven't even been to seminary yet."

Paul laughed. "You wouldn't be licensed at first, of course. And you would be closely monitored. But you could hold Sunday services for the members of my little church while doing what you do best—charitable work with the people."

Could it be possible? Was this God's plan all along?

"Perhaps the Lord has raised you up for just this time, Jimmy. It's hard to get a pastor willing to take over a ministry such as this. The thought of leaving these dear folks with no one to lead them nearly broke my heart. If I knew you were here, it would be a great weight off my mind." He smiled. "Of course, you realize there's not much monetary compensation. A small stipend. And you probably wouldn't get that at first."

"That wouldn't matter. I can work on the docks part-time."

Paul nodded then sighed. "If you marry, it won't be easy. A wife has to have the same calling in order for it to work."

Jimmy jumped up, laughing. "I haven't told you, but I'm engaged to be married. To the sweetest girl—Cecilia Willow."

"That is exciting news. Congratulations. Would Miss Willow, by any chance, be Rev. Willow's daughter?" He rubbed his hands together, grinning. "That's just like God, isn't it? He's brought you the perfect mate."

❧

Jimmy headed toward the cargo ship where he was working today and reflected on Paul's remark. The perfect mate. It was true. His heart said so. He hadn't seen Cici since her strange declaration. She had asked him not to press her just now, promising to tell him everything on Saturday.

He sighed. Two more days. Well, she was worth waiting for, and whatever this mysterious upset in their relationship was, he was determined it could and would be overcome. Now that he knew in his heart that Cici loved him and loved the ministry he was called to, nothing would tear them apart.

"Jimmy." He turned and saw Patrick and several other boys trailing down the street carrying what looked to be wet cats.

"Hey, what are you boys up to?" Satisfaction swept over him. Most of the children looked better these days. Still dirty and ragged, but their cheeks had color and their ribs weren't showing. Between the soup kitchen and the food boxes, they'd lost the defiant, angry look a lot of them had carried. It was hard to be happy when you were hungry. Now if they could get enough spiritual food, everything would be fine.

"Aw, we just found these cats in a sack in the river. Must have just been throwed in 'cause they were all alive. They sure were scared though."

Jimmy winced. "Yeah, I'll bet. They were lucky you found them. But don't make a practice of going into the river."

"Aw, whatcha think we are, nuts?" Tony, an older boy scowled. "Who'd wanta swim in that dirty old sewer?"

Jimmy laughed. "I guess you're right. I won't worry then."

They waved and walked away.

What could he do about getting them to church? He'd like to take them with him, but it was too far for them to walk. Well, if he did get the church here, as Paul thought was very possible, he'd do everything he could to persuade them to come on Sunday mornings.

The *Eastland* was just pulling into harbor when Jimmy's shift ended. He shaded his eyes and tried to catch a glimpse of Cobb. True to his word, he had shown up at church the last two Sundays. He'd also bought a Bible, and when the *Eastland* was in, the two of them had studied together during their midday break. Now that Cobb had a taste of God's Word, he seemed hungry for more.

Jimmy was thankful to God for that and for his love for Cici and the ministry. If only Sutton hadn't shown up again, life would be a beautiful thing.

"Waaahooo!" Jimmy grinned at the sound of Cobb's

familiar yell. He ran down the *Eastland*'s gangplank and took a wide jump onto the dock.

Jimmy grinned and waved. "Hey. How long are you in for?"

"Just tonight. We're one of the boats the Western Electric bunch chartered for their picnic in Indiana." He whistled. "Company must be loaded. Five charters for a picnic."

"Five? Must be quite a crowd." Jimmy leaned against a post.

"Must be. The *Eastland* alone holds around twenty-six hundred." Cobb shook his head. "Sure glad I won't be cooking lunch for all those folks."

Jimmy wrinkled his brow. "Why do you need to go, then?"

"Some of them will be wanting breakfast. And probably sandwiches and stuff on the way back." He nodded. "Don't worry. They'll keep me busy."

Jimmy laughed and clapped him on the back. "I gotta get home. Maybe I'll see you later."

"Not if I see you first." Cobb laughed and waved. "Hey, Jimbo, wait a minute."

Jimmy turned.

"Just wanted you to know. . .had a serious talk with Jesus the other day." A grin split Cobb's glowing face. "He's my Savior now."

❧

"Are you serious?" Danni's squeal of joy shot through Jimmy's head and he flinched back against the parlor sofa, even while he grinned and nodded.

"I never expected that. I didn't." She shook her head and her face shone. "God, forgive me, I didn't expect that."

"Yeah, but you haven't been around Cobb lately. He's a changed man."

"I am awed at God's might and goodness." She leaned back in her chair, pressing her hand to her back, then propped her feet back up on the little footstool. She poked her needle into the pillowcase she was embroidering. "Hmm. Maybe he'll be a good influence on Sutton."

"Don't count on it." Jimmy narrowed his eyes. He had forgiven Sutton—at least he was almost sure he had—and maybe he could even forget if not for the new threat against Danni.

"Jimmy"—Danni's voice was low and soft—"no one is beyond God's grace and mercy. All he would need to do is surrender, and God could change him in a second." She sat there quietly, so sweet and sincere.

Jimmy's heart stirred. Would things change between him and Danni when he got married? He took a deep breath. Of course they would. There was a lot of change when she married Blake. But it wasn't a bad thing at all. Simply different. Now she was going to be a mother. They were grown up. They didn't need each other the same way they had when they were children. "Danni." He paused.

"Yes, little brother?" She grinned.

He grinned back. "Nothing. Just thinking." *Let's stay close, Danni. Let's always stay close.*

"I'm praying for Cici." Her tone grew serious. "I don't know what's wrong. But I know she loves you. And she's a sweet girl. You should see her at the soup kitchen. Everyone loves her, especially the children."

He nodded. "She promised to explain Saturday. I hope I'm busy tomorrow so I can keep my mind off it."

"You'll be fine. You're a strong man." She started. "Oh."

"What?" Jimmy jumped up. "Are you all right, sis?"

She waved her hand and flinched. "I'm fine. Junior is making his presence known. Sit down, for heaven's sake, Jimmy. You should be used to it by now."

He flopped down on his chair. "Don't scare me like that."

She threw him a tender smile. "Thanks for caring about me."

"Junior is going to be a lucky little boy to have a mother like you."

"Oh really?" She tilted her head to one side. "And what if

Junior should turn out to be a little girl, Uncle Jimmy?"

He grinned. "Then she'll be the luckiest young lady who ever lived."

"Let's stay close, Jimmy. Promise me. No matter what, we'll always love each other just like we always have."

"Always."

&

Cici paced her bedroom floor. Was she making a mistake? Confronting Sutton had seemed like a good idea, but now she wasn't so sure. After the things Jimmy had told her, it was obvious the man was dangerous. But he was older now. How dangerous could he be?

A laugh turned into a hiccup. She cleared her throat. She had made up her mind. She wouldn't back out now. And the deck would be teeming with people. What could he do? She tossed her curls and sat on the chair by her lace-curtained window.

Should she tell someone? But that person would only try to stop her from going through with it. She straightened her neck and lifted her chin. She wouldn't be a coward and back out now. She would do this for Jimmy and Danni. When Sutton realized he was exposed, he'd give up his evil plan, whatever it might be. The night was half gone before Cici finally dropped off to sleep.

She woke with a start. Jumping out of bed, she switched on the light and peered at the clock by her bed. Six o'clock. She'd need to hurry. When she got to the kitchen, she was met by the aroma of apples and cinnamon wafting up from a bubbling pot of oatmeal.

"I know you're in a hurry, Cecilia, but you need to eat a bite before you go to the docks."

She complied, happy that her mother assumed she was headed for the soup kitchen. And she did plan to go there as soon as she'd talked to Sutton.

"Good morning, daughter." Papa laid his paper down and

turned up his cheek for her kiss.

"Good morning, Papa." She grabbed his coffee mug. "Here, let me fill this for you."

Everything seemed surreal as she hurried through breakfast, washed her dishes in the kitchen sink, and kissed her folks good-bye.

The Clark Street Bridge was crowded with carriages and automobiles, probably filled with the picnic-going employees and their families headed to the boats. The streetcar clacked past them on the center rails.

Cici got off and adjusted her hat to protect against the light mist that had begun. Five chartered boats were lined up and there must have been thousands of people boarding. She frowned. Was the *Eastland* leaning? It appeared lopsided. She shook her head. Her imagination, of course.

She glanced around trying to catch a glimpse of Gail in the crowd but didn't see her. She slipped between two quarreling children and was shoved aside by a large woman carrying a birdcage. Her glance slid up the side of the *Eastland* to the crowded deck. It would be just like Gail to be on board already even though she'd promised to meet her on the dock.

Her gaze brushed across the mob and she inhaled a sharp breath. Sutton stood by the rail looking down. His eyes met hers and he smiled and motioned upward. A dark-haired girl stood just behind him. Was that Gail? She couldn't see her clearly, but it must be.

She glanced toward the gangplank. The crowd had thinned and a short line was all that remained to board. Should she? It wasn't too late to change her mind.

She reached into her jacket pocket for the handwritten ticket Gail had given her. Lifting her chin, she took a deep breath and stepped toward the *Eastland*'s crowded gangplank.

nineteen

"Cici!" Jimmy let the door of the employee shack bang shut behind him and rushed across the dock toward the *Eastland*. Cici was halfway up the gangplank. He'd know those curls and that walk anywhere.

"Cici!" His shout went unheard.

An orchestra played on the promenade deck and some of the passengers were dancing. Voices clamored and deckhands tried to shout to each other above the music. The noise drowned out Jimmy's call. He stopped and exhaled a huff of air. The gangplank was being pulled into the *Eastland*. The *Theodore Roosevelt* and one other boat were still loading passengers, and they called out to one another, adding to the clamor.

Jimmy scanned the *Eastland*'s deck, hoping to catch Cici's eye. Why would she have boarded? Did someone invite her on the excursion? She hadn't mentioned it. Jimmy frowned as the *Eastland* listed to portside. Soon it righted and he breathed a sigh of relief.

A man stood at the edge of the wharf, frowning toward the listing boat. Several people stood at the rail, laughing and shouting for him to come on aboard. Suddenly he jumped across the water and his friends helped him over the rail. Crazy people.

Jimmy's gaze swept the crowd on deck again. There she was, and there. . . Jimmy's heart froze. Sutton. What was she doing with Sutton? They faced each other, seeming not to notice the people who crowded around them at the rail. Why hadn't she told him she knew Sutton? Was she involved with him in some way? Surely not. They hadn't acknowledged

149

each other at the theater that night. But maybe. No. He wouldn't believe for a moment that Cici would be involved in a plot against Danni.

A couple of women crowded in front of them, and when they moved, there was no sign of Cici or Sutton. Jimmy shaded his eyes to see if he could spot Cobb aboard, but he was probably in the galley.

Fear clutched his chest. If Cici wasn't involved with Sutton, and he was certain she wasn't, then she must be in some sort of trouble. Should he inform the harbor authorities? But what would he say to them? His fiancée was on the ship with another man? They'd laugh, more than likely. He turned and headed for the *Theodore Roosevelt* to help set the gangplank in place. There was nothing he could do.

But he could pray and trust God.

☙

Cici shoved her way across the crowded deck. There he was, and Gail stood beside him. She'd give her an earful as soon as—

Fear stabbed her at the glint of satisfaction in Sutton's eyes. Why had she thought this was a good idea? She darted a hopeful glance at Gail, but the girl gave her an apologetic shrug and rushed toward the gangplank.

Cici started to turn and felt herself jerked backward. Before she could scream, Sutton yanked her to his side so tightly she gasped. She struggled to no avail against his deathlike grip. Pain stabbed her as something hard was pressed against her ribs.

"Be a nice girl and you might get off this boat alive, my dear." Sutton's hot breath blew against her neck as he whispered into her ear, "I would be devastated if I had to shoot you."

She opened her mouth to scream, but a jab from the gun caused her breath to catch in her throat. Who would hear her over the orchestra anyway?

He maneuvered her to a short flight of steps and guided her down to the deserted deck below.

She struggled as he half carried, half shoved her down a narrow hall. Suddenly she lost her balance as the boat rocked from side to side.

Sutton grabbed her and pushed her into a tiny alcove. He was quiet for a moment then shrugged.

"Nothing to be afraid of. The boat is merely listing. Now, Cici, dear, listen closely, for I'll only say it once. If you wish to get off this ship alive and see dear Jimmy again, you had best go quietly the rest of the way."

"But where are you taking me?" Her voice trembled. This was not the way she'd planned things. "And why are you doing this?"

He gave a short laugh and drew her closer to his side. "Because, my dear, I want young Jimmy and the abominable Blake Nelson to know what it's like to lose something they hold dear."

"But. . ."

"Enough." He gave her a slight shove and they started down the hall once more. He stopped at a door, unlocked it, and threw it open, revealing a medium-sized stateroom.

Cici gasped. Fear pierced through her. The room was dark except for a small lamp. She had hoped there might be someone there who would help her, but there was not a soul in the cabin. "No. I'm not going in there."

Laughing, Sutton gave her a shove.

Cici stumbled through the door and watched in horror as he closed it behind him.

"Don't look so frightened, my dear. I'm not a monster." He laid the gun on a small table and removed his coat. His dark eyes devoured her for a moment. Then he went to a small sideboard and poured wine into two glasses. He held one out to her.

"No." She shoved it away. "You know I don't drink."

He shrugged and tipped the glass up, downing the liquid,

then placed it on the counter. "Sit down, my dear. You may as well relax. You're not going anywhere."

"I don't understand why you would do this." A shuddering motion told her the boat was pulling away from the dock. Hot tears rushed to her eyes and she blinked them back. "The ship is leaving. Please let me go, Sutton."

Sutton shook his head. "No. You're not going anywhere. For then my plan would be spoiled, you see. But you still don't understand. They must not have told you the story of how I was robbed of the lovely Danielle. Sit down." He motioned to a small sofa.

"I'd rather stand." Cici pressed her lips together and threw him what she hoped was a determined glare.

He sighed. "I said sit." He shoved her onto the sofa and sat beside her. "So you wish to know why I must have my revenge." He leaned back and narrowed his eyes. "Danielle Grayson was the most beautiful woman I ever knew. She was ten years old the first time I laid eyes on her. Even then I knew she was special, with red curls wild around her tiny head and green eyes that flashed and sparkled. As she grew up, her beauty overwhelmed me. And not only her physical beauty. She was graceful and gentle, always caring about those around her. Especially her little lame brother. I kept her close, not sending her out on the streets with the other children. She did chores around the house and I even brought a tutor in for her and Jimmy."

He took a long drink then sighed. "I knew if I was ever to have a chance with her, I must be kind to Jimmy. She adored him and was always very protective." Sutton's words slurred and his eyes were wild.

Cici squirmed and moved farther away from him.

He reached out and grabbed her wrist. "Don't try it." Pain filled his voice as he continued. "Then she spurned me." The man was either drunk or mad, and he hadn't had that much to drink. "To teach her a lesson, I sent her out with some of the boys to do a job."

His breath came in rapid gasps and he leaned back and ran his hand over his eyes. "Something went wrong. The boys got away, but she was caught. Somehow she managed to talk her way out of it. She always was a good little actress." Bitterness filled his voice. "As she showed me well. Lying to me. Making me think she was still part of our little family while all the time she plotted to betray me. She was in love with someone else. She came home to try to talk me into letting Jimmy go. The police raided, and thanks to Danielle Grayson, the one love of my life, the one intended for me, I was sent to prison and my little family was scattered."

"You were a criminal, Sutton." Cici almost shouted the words. "What did you expect? You taught innocent children to steal and made them think it was all right. Family? You only used them."

His eyes darkened in anger and he raised his hand then lowered it. "No, I took care of them. They were my children."

She jumped up. "Let me go, Sutton. You're insane. You're never going to have Danielle. She loves her husband and they're going to have a child."

He jumped up, eyes filled with rage. "No. . .Jimmy Grayson will know what it feels like for the woman he loves to be claimed by another. And his pain will be hers. She will see what she has driven me to. And through her, that seducing husband of hers will suffer."

Fear gripped Cici as he lunged for her. Then the floor fell away and she began to slide. She screamed.

The ship had turned onto its side. It must be sinking.

A table flew through the air and hit Sutton's head. Blood gushed. His lifeless body tumbled head over heels toward the door, where water had begun to seep in.

Cici screamed again, continuing to slide toward the wall. Suddenly the boat listed more and she fell, grasping for something to stop her plunge. She hit the wall hard and something exploded in her elbow.

God, help me.

ða

She was innocent. She must be. There was no way Jimmy would believe Cici was mixed up with Sutton and his plots. But then, why was she with him? Was this what she had to tell him? Something about Sutton?

Shouts broke into his thoughts as he swabbed down the dock. Probably some of the dockhands roughhousing. He straightened his back and glanced around. He drew his breath in sharply. No. No. He stood still, too stunned to move, not believing what he saw. Not more than forty feet from the wharf, the *Eastland* lay halfway on her side and continued to roll as she sank into the river.

Dear God, Cici.

He dropped the heavy mop and ran. At the edge of the wharf, he stood transfixed. The *Eastland* groaned and then came to rest on its side. The water was thick with passengers and crew swimming toward land. Jimmy looked over the mob frantically, trying to locate Cici.

Yanking off his boots, he jumped in, barely missing a man and a woman who clung together as they made their way to the dock. He swam toward the ship, shoving people aside as he went. The one thought that went through his mind was Cici, trapped in the boat.

A man with two children clinging to his shoulders bumped against him, his eyes pleading for help. Jimmy pulled one of the children from the man's back and swam back to the dock, where someone took the child. Then he turned and headed back toward the ship. How much time had passed? He swam on through bodies, some coughing, some screaming and kicking. But where was Cici?

Oh God, please don't let her be below deck.

The steamer had sunk so fast, there wouldn't have been time for her to get up the stairs. She could be trapped beneath the water. She could be dead by now.

A loose lifeboat bobbed on top of the water. A young boy

scrambled over the side and fell into it.

Almost to the boat, Jimmy jerked as someone, gasping, grabbed him from behind. He struggled but couldn't get loose from the arms entwined around his neck. He felt himself sinking and drew in a deep breath. He tried to kick his way back up to the surface, but the arms tightened in a near stranglehold. His mind and body cried out for air.

Suddenly the choking arms fell away. Kicking, Jimmy fought his way upward toward the precious air. Blackness threatened and he knew he couldn't make it.

Lord Jesus, receive my spirit and please save Cici.

Something grabbed him and he felt himself floating upward. Blackness overcame him.

≈

Cici struggled to shove Sutton's body away from the door. Pain stabbed her elbow, but it was lessening. She must have hit a nerve. Thank the Lord it wasn't broken. Tugging and pushing at Sutton's body, she finally moved him away from the door. After working at it for a few minutes, she managed to pull it open and fell through, landing against the wall beyond. She glanced around, trying to think what to do.

Water was coming in at one end of the corridor. She was alone but could hear screams from above and below. A sob caught in her throat. What should she do? The stairs were farther down, but that was where the water was coming in. She needed to get to a higher place.

Turning, she saw the side rails, which were now going upward toward the side that was above the water. Her heart pounded and dizziness overcame her. She had to keep focused. Grabbing the rail, she pulled herself onto an overturned table then forced herself to climb onto anything she could get a foothold on.

The sound of pounding came from above her.

She cried out, "Help! I'm down here!"

At another noise behind her, she turned. Water was filling

the corridor. Objects bobbed up and down in it.

Cici gasped. She must get higher.

What had she been thinking to confront Sutton alone? She scrambled frantically upward, grabbing at swinging doors and rails to haul herself up. Her progress was slow and the water rose steadily.

Would Jimmy be among the rescuers? *Lord, please save me. But if I'm to die, please don't let Jimmy find my body. And please comfort him and Mama and Papa.*

She heard drilling above her. Oh, if only they could get through before it was too late.

Something touched her foot. She jerked it up then glanced behind her. Sutton's body floated on top of the water, which was now just below her. Fear and nausea washed over her. Once more she started to climb. Toward safety. Toward people who were attempting to get through to her. She must reach the top.

twenty

"Jimbo, Jimbo, wake up. Come on, Jimmy."

Something slapped Jimmy's face, hard, and he heard Cobb's voice as if from a distance. He blinked and opened his eyes.

Cobb was bombarding his face with one slap after another.

Jimmy grabbed his wrist. "Okay, I'm awake." But why was he lying on the dock, soaking wet? He sat up and shook his head, water flying from his hair. He blinked. Cici. The boat had gone down. He struggled to get up.

Cobb grabbed his arm and yanked him to his feet. "I saw the guy pull you under." Cobb's eyes were wide. "Didn't think I'd ever find you."

Jimmy grabbed him by his shoulders. "Have you seen Cici?" The torment in his mind sounded in his voice.

"Cici? No. Why?" He threw a puzzled glance at Jimmy. "Maybe you better sit down."

"No. Cici was on the *Eastland*. We've got to find her." He pulled his arm loose and ran barefoot to the edge of the wharf, where he stood in horror.

Bodies floated in the water, bumping against each other. Cries came from the living trying to make their way to shore. Divers avoided the still forms, focusing their efforts on pulling the living from the river.

A grating, screaming sound jerked Jimmy's attention to the above-water portion of the steamer. Rescue workers with drills knelt on the exposed side, trying to remove the side plates. He took a deep breath to prepare for the cold water.

Cobb grabbed him. "Wait, I'll go with you." He squeezed Jimmy's arm. "We'll find her, pal. I promise."

Slowly they made their way through the water, checking each female body that floated by.

Jimmy had a strong feeling that Cici was trapped inside the steamer. "I'm going to dive below and see if I can see inside the portholes."

"No, wait. You're still weak from lack of oxygen. I'll go. Keep looking around through the bodies."

Jimmy knew if Cici was trapped inside the submerged side, it would be no use. There was no chance anyone could be alive underwater that long.

A shout went up. Jimmy looked up and saw a rescue worker pulling someone, alive, through an opening. His heart lurched, and he swam toward the outer rails. He grabbed the bottom one and started up.

"I'm right behind you, Jimbo." Cobb's welcome voice was like velvet to his ears.

"You didn't see her?"

"Couldn't see anything down there. I'm sorry."

Jimmy hauled himself up and peered around. Two women and several crying, frightened children were being loaded onto stretchers.

Jimmy walked over and looked down at one of the women. "Do you know Cici Willow? Blond curls, very young and pretty. Did you see her?"

She groaned and shook her head. The other woman couldn't offer any help either. Two of the rescuers were pulling someone from another hole in the ship. This time a young girl, followed by a middle-aged man.

Something pounded beneath Jimmy's feet. "Hey, over here. Someone's down there."

In a short time, the flap was cut away. Jimmy peered around the workers and his heart jumped at the sight of blond curls. He groaned when the woman turned her face upward. Not Cici.

Dear God, please let her be alive. And help us to find her.

"Over here! Someone help me get this woman out of here. She's stuck or something."

☙

Pain seared through Cici's leg as she tugged to try to get free. Somewhere in the dark water that now reached her waist, her foot was caught. A heavy chest had slammed against the wall, pinning her foot and lower leg. Tears of frustration stained her cheeks as she stared up at the rescue worker. She shook her head. "I can't move it."

"Cici!" Jimmy shoved the man away and reached for her.

She reached her arms up to him. "Oh, Jimmy." She gazed into his wonderful face. The face she'd feared she'd never see again. "My foot is wedged tight. I can't get out." Panic clutched tight at her chest and throat. Was she going to die when she was so close to being with him once more? Water rushed around her waist, lapping at the walls and everything it touched.

"Sweetheart, I'll get you out. I promise. Try not to panic." He turned. "Cobb, grab a rope, okay?"

In less than a minute, Jimmy handed the end of a rope down to her. "Cici, I want you to tie this around your waist. Make sure you get it tight enough that it won't come loose. Can you do that?"

She nodded and wrapped the rope around her waist twice, then tied it in a knot. She gave it a tug to be sure then nodded to Jimmy.

"Now, honey, you're going to have to trust us, okay?"

"I trust you, Jimmy." And she did. More than she'd ever trusted anyone. Even though her heart pounded against her chest and her throat was constricted with fear, she trusted him.

He turned and spoke to the men behind him, then turned back to her. "Honey, I want you to try to lower yourself into the water so I can get through to help you."

Panic pierced her heart and her breathing came in short

gasps. She hung on to Jimmy's hands and shook her head. "I can't."

The choked whisper must have reached him, because pain clouded his eyes. "Yes, you can. Three strong men are holding on to the rope. They won't let you go. I promise, sweetheart. Please. We have to get you out of there. The water will continue to rise. Don't you see?"

She glanced down. The water was still at her waist, but it did seem a little higher. She bit her lip and nodded. "All right, Jimmy."

She swallowed past the sudden lump in her throat, slid one hand out of his, and grabbed the rope just above her waist. Taking a deep breath she let go with the other. She sank to her chin and water whipped around her shoulders and neck. "Jimmy!" Angry waves of water swirled around her and she held on to the rope with both hands, making sure the knot at her waist wasn't coming loose. The light from outside disappeared and terror beat at her as she fought the watery darkness.

Then light streamed in once more and Jimmy's arms were around her, holding her close. "It's all right, sweetheart. I'm with you. I'll get you out of here." He pulled back and looked into her eyes. "I have to go under the water to get you loose. Don't be afraid. I won't be long." Then he was gone, beneath the dark evil that waited to devour them both.

No, I won't think like that. God is taking care of us. He sent Jimmy and the other men, and He'll save us from this.

Pain shot through her ankle and up her leg as the chest shifted. Where was Jimmy? It was taking too long. Another shift and suddenly her foot was free.

Jimmy bobbed up beside her, coughing and gasping. He looked into her eyes and grinned. "Let's get out of here."

With Jimmy lifting and Cobb pulling, Cici crawled out through the hole in the side of the ship, ignoring the throbbing pain in her leg and foot. Cobb lifted her up and put his arm around her shoulders, supporting her until Jimmy stood beside them.

They fell into each other's arms. Cici basked in Jimmy's kisses and the sweet words he whispered in her ears.

"Uh, excuse me, miss. We need to get you to the hospital." The emergency worker stood grinning, with a stretcher at his feet and another grinning man at the other end of it.

"Jimmy, I want to go home."

"Now, sweetheart, we need to get that ankle taken care of and make sure you're okay after being in the water for so long."

"Will you come with me?" She was acting like a baby, but she didn't care.

He picked her up and laid her on the stretcher. "Just let anyone try to keep me from it." His lips brushed against hers.

She closed her eyes and dizziness engulfed her. She needed to tell him something. But what? Oh. Sutton. Then darkness came.

❧

Jimmy stumbled into the house, exhaustion in every muscle of his body.

He'd stayed at the hospital for nearly two hours waiting for Cici to awake. The doctor had assured them there was nothing wrong with her except exhaustion and a bruised ankle. The minute her eyes had opened, she'd motioned him close.

"Sutton. . ." She took a deep breath. "He's dead, Jimmy."

A surge of relief shot through Jimmy. The lifting of the burden he'd carried so long swept over him in a lightness very near dizziness. But almost immediately remorse stabbed through him. How could he be happy with the news of someone's death when the man didn't know Jesus?

"Cici, are you sure?" But she had fallen back asleep. He brushed his lips across her forehead and whispered good-bye to her parents.

Jimmy had made a quick trip to the house to tell Blake and Danni the news, and after making sure Danni was all right, he and Blake had gone to help with the rescue attempts.

He'd stayed until darkness was so thick there was no possibility of saving even one more person. He shuddered at the memory of row after row of sheet-wrapped bodies lying on the floor of the makeshift morgue at the Reid Murdoch plant. He didn't think he'd ever forget the feel of those waterlogged bodies as he helped load them onto trucks later for transport to the armory.

"Jimmy"—Danni stood in the parlor doorway—"come in and put your feet up. You look like you're about to pass out."

"I'm too dirty, so I'd better not. I'll ruin the furniture." But the sight of the overstuffed chair by the window drew him and he took a step forward.

"Nonsense. Get in here." She peered into his eyes, then gave a little gasp and wrapped her arms around him.

"Oh, Jimmy, I'm so sorry. It must have been horrible out there." She released him then guided him to the chair.

"It was terrible. Danni, you wouldn't believe it." He dropped onto the soft cushion and buried his face in his hands. Sobs wracked his body. Sobs that had a life of their own and would not be stopped.

Her comforting hands patted his shoulder then brushed his hair from his eyes.

Finally, he sat up straight. "Thanks, Danni. I haven't cried like that since I was a kid."

"It's all right. There's nothing wrong with a man crying, and you have plenty to cry about."

"I need to get cleaned up and back to the hospital."

"Mrs. Willow sent a message a little while ago. She said to tell you Cici is at home and sleeping like a baby. Cici asked her to tell you to please get some rest and come see her in the morning."

"But you're sure she's all right?" She'd been so pale when he kissed her good-bye.

"I'm sure. Mrs. Willow said all Cici could talk about was how brave you were and how proud she was that you went back to do your part to help." She brushed his hair back, a motion he'd resent any other time. "How about something to eat?"

He shook his head. "There were volunteers handing out food and drinks all day. I'm not hungry. Is Blake asleep?" He probably was. Blake wasn't used to long hours of physical labor but had worked tirelessly alongside Jimmy and the other volunteers most of the day and into the early hours of the night. He'd only left because he didn't want to leave Danni alone in the house.

"Yes, he was so tired he took a short bath and fell across the bed. I don't think he's moved since."

He reached up and touched her cheek. "Danni, are you okay?"

Her face paled, but she smiled then reached over and placed her hand on his arm. "I'm fine. Go on upstairs and get some rest."

Jimmy nodded and headed up the stairs. He'd take a long hot bath and go to bed. He only hoped his dreams would be sweet ones of Cici and not nightmares of the scenes he'd witnessed today.

≈

Jimmy tapped on the parsonage door, the sound blending in with the pelting of the rain against the roof and sidewalk. In a moment, the door flew open and Mrs. Willow beamed at him from the foyer.

"Come in, my boy, before you get soaked." She took his umbrella and placed it in the stand.

"I hope you don't mind my early intrusion." Jimmy loosened the knot in his tie, which seemed about to choke him. "I wanted to look in on Cici before church."

"No, it's not too early. She's in the parlor. Go right in. I have to finish making salad and put the roast in the oven before church." She smiled and stepped into the dining room.

Jimmy walked into the parlor and stopped.

Cici sat on the sofa, her foot and ankle wrapped and resting on a footstool, her head bent over the Bible in her lap. Golden curls fell forward and rested on each side of her face. No girl was ever this beautiful. She glanced up, and when she saw him, her face lit up and she smiled. "Jimmy, come sit by me. Are you rested? It must have been awful."

"I'm quite rested." He sat beside her and ran his thumb down her cheek, concerned that she was still wan. "How is your ankle?"

"Oh, there's some swelling and it's tender, but I'm fine. Mother put ice on it. And the doctor said I was fine. Not a thing wrong." She sighed. "He said to stay off it for a few days, so Mama won't let me go to church."

He took her hand in his. "I was so afraid when the boat went down."

Confusion slid across her face. "How did you know I was on it?"

"I saw you boarding. I called, but there was such a din of noise, you couldn't hear." He had so many questions to ask. Why was she on the *Eastland*? How did she know Sutton? What was it she wanted to tell him? But all he could do was gaze at her and thank God she was safe.

She bit her lip, and her hand, resting in his, trembled. "Jimmy, there's something I have to tell you."

"What is it, dearest? You can tell me anything." And almost anything would be better than this doubt and worry.

"Jimmy, it's time to go." Mrs. Willow stood in the doorway pinning her hat. She sent a beaming smile their way.

Jimmy sighed. Whatever she had to tell him would have to wait until after church.

twenty-one

"Over eight hundred known dead so far?" Jimmy shook his head in disbelief and groaned. "They were so close to the harbor. It seems unbelievable."

"I know, son. A horrible tragedy." Rev. Willow leaned forward in the wingback chair in the parlor. "And they still have no idea what caused it."

They'd all come into the parlor after dinner. The horrors the city had faced seemed to be the only topic on their minds. The church congregation had been in a state of shock. It seemed everyone knew someone who knew someone who had died on the *Eastland*.

"According to the newspapers, they're still pulling bodies from the ship." Cici's voice caught in a sob and she jumped up.

"Cecilia, dear, I think you should lie down for a while. You're very pale." Mrs. Willow leaned over and touched Cici's forehead.

"I'm all right, Mama." She smiled and pressed her mother's hand. The next moment she swayed. Jimmy caught her before she hit the floor.

Mr. Willow took his daughter from Jimmy's arms. "I'll take her upstairs. Apparently she should have stayed in bed today."

"But should we call the doctor?" Jimmy glanced frantically from Cici to her father.

Mrs. Willow placed her hand on his arm. "She'll be fine, son. She just overdid it. Go home and get some rest. I promise we'll take good care of her. See, she's coming around already."

Sure enough, Cici's eyes had opened. "I'm sorry, Jimmy.

We'll talk tomorrow. I promise."

"It's all right, sweetheart." He glanced at her father, took a deep breath, and leaned over and kissed her cheek. "Are you sure you'll be okay?"

"I'm sure. I just need to rest."

Jimmy headed home, disappointment in missing their talk all mixed up with concern for her health and joy in her changed demeanor today. She'd seemed humble, with a seriousness in her smile that hadn't been there before.

When Jimmy arrived at home, he said a quick hello to Danni and Blake and went upstairs to change. They probably needed volunteers at the dock, so he'd decided on the way home to see what he could do to help. He came back down and leaned against the parlor door. "I'm heading down to the dock to see if I can help for a few hours."

"Wait a minute, Jimmy. I'll go with you." Blake set his coffee cup down and gave Danni a hug. "Just give me a minute to change."

When they got to the docks, it was almost a repeat of the day before. Except that now everyone who was being pulled out of the water was dead.

Cobb stood next to a body, his hand over his face. It had to be Sutton for Cobb to be grieving so.

Jimmy hurried over to Cobb and squeezed his shoulder.

Cobb stared at Sutton's body. "They found him in one of the hallways. It looked like he died from a blow to the head."

"I'm sorry, Cobb. At least it was sudden. He didn't suffer." And he was sorry. Sorry for Cobb's grief.

❧

Jimmy sat once more in Blake and Danni's parlor. The senior Nelsons and Pops were there, and the Kramers had also joined them. It was good to have family at a time like this. They'd all been worried about what Sutton might do.

"So now the blighter's gone. He won't be bringin' grief to this family." Pops voiced what they were all secretly feeling.

"But Pops"—Danni wiped her eyes—"Sutton wasn't a Christian."

"Now how would you be knowing that, lass?" Pops turned a stern eye on her. "Were you a wee fly on the wall before he went to his watery grave? Maybe he had a chance to call on the Lord and ask forgiveness."

Danni's tear-filled eyes lit with a gleam of hope. "Do you think so, Pops?"

"Now, now, I know you're worrying in that tender heart of yours. But you just have to leave the man in God's hands." Pops reached over and patted her shoulder.

"Mr. O'Shannon is absolutely right, Danielle." Mrs. Kramer, who had taken Danni under her wing eight years ago, smiled at her now. "God's business is God's business. Our business is with the living. And there will be plenty of those who need our help, especially now."

Danni nodded. "You're right, I know that."

Once more a pang of remorse shot through Jimmy. *God, forgive me. I'm not sorry that Sutton is dead. He can't hurt Danni now. Or anyone else. Change my heart, Lord.*

Mr. Nelson turned to Jimmy. "How are your little friends in the tenements, my boy?"

Jimmy's heart lurched. He had been so focused on the disaster and Cici that he hadn't seen the children in a couple of days, except to send them away from the docks after the *Eastland* went down. He'd waved them away several times during the day and early evening. "They were pretty shook up yesterday. I intended to check on them all today to find out how they were handling things. Then when I saw Sutton, I forgot." He shook his head.

"Well, that's understandable. Don't beat yourself up over it."

"Thank you, sir. I won't. I guess now that everyone is here, it would be a good time for me to tell you my plans." He glanced around.

Mrs. Kramer sat on a dainty chair with her husband

standing behind her, his hand resting on her shoulder. Mrs. Nelson, seated next to her husband, sent Jimmy an encouraging smile. Pops leaned forward. Blake and Danni waited, their eyes expectant.

"I'm definitely entering seminary next month. Pastor Paul and Rev. Willow have both agreed to sponsor me, and they feel sure I'll be allowed to minister in a layperson's position at the chapel Paul is leaving. I'll have to work part-time at the docks because I'll only be receiving a small stipend, but I'm sure I can earn enough to support us."

"You know very well you can count on us for help, Jimmy." Danni's eyes held concern, but she'd finally accepted his choice.

"I know, sis, but I believe if I do my best and trust in the Lord, He'll take care of me. His Word promises that." He smiled. "I know you have big faith. Can't you trust Him with me, too?"

She brushed tears away and hugged him. "Okay, little brother. I guess I can stop trying to be your mother now." She sniffled. "But I'll still cook for you until you get married."

Jimmy grinned and stood. "That's a relief. I thought I might be overdoing the independence thing. And now, I hate to leave good company, but my fiancée is waiting."

❧

Pain and dread hit Cici's heart as Jimmy walked into the parlor. If only he still loved her after she told him everything. She managed a smile. "Jimmy, would you mind helping me out to the porch swing? I've been inside too long, and I need fresh air."

"I'd be happy to." He helped her to stand on one foot, and she managed to walk and hop out to the porch. The rain had stopped, but the air was still damp, so Cici drew her shawl around her shoulders.

How she wished she could snuggle close to Jimmy and feel his arms around her. But that wouldn't be fair. He had a right to know first. He had a right to choose whether to love her or not.

All right. *Help me, Father, please. I know You have forgiven me. Please let Jimmy forgive me, too.*

"Cici"—he brushed his hand across her cheek—"don't be afraid to tell me. Whatever it is, it won't change the way I feel for you."

"Oh, Jimmy, I pray that's true. But I won't hold you to it. You see, I've been living a double life." She could barely choke out the words. How could she bear to say more?

"In what way, sweetheart?" Why was he so calm? He didn't even sound surprised.

"You see, a few months ago I met a girl named Gail. She was exciting and full of adventure. I'd never met anyone like her." She cleared her throat. "I'm not saying she persuaded me. I've always had a little bit of a rebellious spirit. Even when I was a little girl, I was naughty."

"All children are naughty sometimes, Cici."

"I know that. But as I grew older, I was very restless. I didn't want to go to church and my friends began to bore me. Even Helen. And we've been best friends all our lives." She lifted her eyes to him. But he only nodded.

"I began spending time with Gail. I met her at Tony's Place and she introduced me to her friends. One of them was James Sutton." She gave Jimmy a quick glance. Surprised that his expression hadn't changed, she cleared her throat. "He seemed very charming. He invited all of us to an evening of dining at the home of one of his wealthy friends. That's where I was going the night you saw me boarding the boat. I lied when I said I was going to see a friend downriver." Heat seared her face as she confessed the lie. But still, he didn't appear shocked at all.

"By then, I was starting to lose some of my awe of my new friends. Most of them drank, and even though I didn't, it bothered me. That night I stayed over at Gail's apartment.

She was drunk and I could hardly stand it." She took a deep breath. "After I knew you loved me and I met your family, I began to pull away from them."

Shame washed over her. "I never should have gotten mixed up with them in the first place. I know that and I'm so terribly sorry. I've repented and I know God has forgiven me."

Jimmy peered into her eyes. "Cici—"

But she stopped him before he could say more. "The night you told me what Sutton had done to you and Danni and so many other children, I decided to face him and convince him to leave you alone. I was so foolish. I thought Gail would be on the boat that night, but it was all a trick to get me on there alone with Sutton. She was one of the children you knew."

"Gail. . . I had hoped she would have gone on to a better life." Jimmy sighed. "But she was very close to Sutton. Like so many of the children. He was their only parent figure."

"A terrible parent figure."

He spoke gently. "Yes, but to children who had never known parents, he was all they had."

Was it possible that he didn't hate her? "Jimmy, I'm so sorry. I love you. That's all I can say." She bowed her head and fought against the desire to throw herself into his arms and beg.

The touch of his hand beneath her chin brought a sigh to her lips, and she closed her eyes. He lifted her chin and she opened her eyes and looked into his. She could hardly breathe. Was that love she saw in his eyes?

He rubbed his thumb across her cheeks and wiped away the tears. "Cici, sweetheart? Did you mean it when you said you loved me?" He gazed into her eyes.

"Of course I did. I love you with all my heart."

"And you want to be my wife, even though you know it will likely be a struggle to do God's work among the poor?"

"Oh yes, I do want that, Jimmy. More than anything. I

love you and I've come to love those poor people. Especially the children. They have good hearts, Jimmy. And they have the right to better lives. And even if you don't want me as your wife, I still intend to work among them in any way I can, because God has called me, too."

Jimmy closed his eyes, and when he opened them they were filled with sheer joy. "My darling Cici, my precious wife to be, with all my heart I want you by my side for the rest of my life."

"And you forgive me?" Wonder filled her heart.

"Sweetheart, the main thing you were guilty of was selfishness, and most of us have been guilty of that. Yes, you were rebellious and made some very bad choices that could have led to terrible things for you, but God has forgiven you. I hold nothing against you. You are my wonderful love. And in my eyes, you've always been wonderful." He brushed his lips across hers. "So—when will you marry me?"

"What?" She laughed. "You want to set a date now?"

"The sooner the better." He grinned. "After all, I'll be moving into Paul's apartment soon and I've never lived alone before."

"Oh, you." She giggled. "How about next summer?"

He frowned. "That's too long. How about Christmas?"

"A Christmas wedding? Really?" Butterflies danced in her stomach. What a wonderful idea.

"Really. What do you think?"

"I think it's a wonderful idea. I'd love a Christmas wedding. But don't think you'll get out of giving me an anniversary gift each year."

"I promise. So it's Christmas, then?" His eyes sparkled with excitement.

"All right. We'd better go tell Mama and Papa."

"Yes, but not just now."

Once more his lips touched hers. Softly at first. Then his kiss deepened and they held each other as if they'd never let go.

A Letter To Our Readers

Dear Reader:

In order that we might better contribute to your reading enjoyment, we would appreciate your taking a few minutes to respond to the following questions. We welcome your comments and read each form and letter we receive. When completed, please return to the following:

Fiction Editor
Heartsong Presents
PO Box 719
Uhrichsville, Ohio 44683

1. Did you enjoy reading *Sugar and Spice* by Frances Devine?
   ❑ Very much! I would like to see more books by this author!
   ❑ Moderately. I would have enjoyed it more if

   _____

   _____

   _____

2. Are you a member of **Heartsong Presents**? ❑ Yes ❑ No
   If no, where did you purchase this book? _____

   _____

3. How would you rate, on a scale from 1 (poor) to 5 (superior), the cover design? _____

4. On a scale from 1 (poor) to 10 (superior), please rate the following elements.

   ____ Heroine   ____ Plot
   ____ Hero   ____ Inspirational theme
   ____ Setting   ____ Secondary characters

5. These characters were special because? _____

_____

_____

6. How has this book inspired your life? _____

_____

_____

7. What settings would you like to see covered in future
   Heartsong Presents books? _____

_____

_____

8. What are some inspirational themes you would like to see
   treated in future books? _____

_____

_____

9. Would you be interested in reading other **Heartsong
   Presents** titles? ❏ Yes ❏ No

10. Please check your age range:

    ❏ Under 18   ❏ 18-24

    ❏ 25-34   ❏ 35-45

    ❏ 46-55   ❏ Over 55

Name _____

Occupation _____

Address _____

City, State, Zip _____

E-mail _____

RODEO HEARTS

THREE-IN-ONE COLLECTION

Saddle up for a rodeo
of romance when three
modern big-city women
meet their matches in
men more comfortable
wearing boots, spurs,
and guns.

Contemporary, paperback, 352 pages, 5¾₆" x 8"

—————————————————————————

HEARTSONG PRESENTS

If you love Christian romance…

$10.99

You'll love Heartsong Presents' inspiring and faith-filled romances by today's very best Christian authors…Wanda E. Brunstetter, Mary Connealy, Susan Page Davis, Cathy Marie Hake, and Joyce Livingston, to mention a few!

When you join Heartsong Presents, you'll enjoy four brand-new, mass market, 176-page books—two contemporary and two historical—that will build you up in your faith when you discover God's role in every relationship you read about!

Imagine…four new romances every four weeks—with men and women like you who long to meet the one God has chosen as the love of their lives…all for the low price of $10.99 postpaid.

To join, simply visit www.heartsong presents.com or complete the coupon below and mail it to the address provided.

Mass Market 176 Pages